After completing her degree in Psychosocial studies with a well-earned 2:1, Claire is currently spending her waking hours split, unevenly, between being a Mother, an Accounts Assistant and a Writer. After the success of her debut novel Twisted Fate and the Nanny Pam children's books with her daughter, she is still tapping away at her keyboard in order to produce more wonderful books for you to enjoy.

Other titles by this author

<u>Novels</u>
Twisted Fate

<u>Children's books</u>
Nanny Pam Takes the Children to Feed the Ducks
Nanny Pam Joins a Band

This book is dedicated to my beautiful Grandaughter who was born on the day this book was finished. Welcome to the world little lady.

And all my dear friends and family who have been unintentionally, yet shamelessly, neglected during the writing of this book. I love you all.

Ups-a-Daisy

❀IN THE BEGINNING❀

Daisy surveyed her appearance in the bedroom mirror. Her blue/green eyes surveying herself critically. She brushed her fringe out of them. It was not a very pleasing sight. She sucked her stomach in, *nope no better*, she stuck it back out and slouched her shoulders further. Why had she left going on the diet so late? She had known about the reunion so far in advance she could have literally transformed herself and healed from the surgery by now. Yet here she stood fat and bedraggled, not to mention stressed and overheating. She had now managed to try on practically every outfit in her wardrobe but to no avail. Nothing seemed to portray the look she was endeavouring to depict. She flopped down on to the edge of the bed and laid back on to the pile of clothes which were now taking up residence there.

Just as the first exasperated sob threatened to escape her chubby frame, a hanger dug itself into her back.

"Ouch," she yelped.

She clambered off and sat on the floor, her back against the bed, her head in her hands. That was the last straw, she allowed herself to just crumble. Something, that if the truth be told, she had been holding back on doing for a few weeks now. Not only had she changed her indecisive mind more times than she could count regarding her attendance at the reunion, but now she had practically thrown herself over the edge by trying to decide what the hell she should wear. Daisy swung round and punched the pile of clothes and swore angrily at the ridiculousness of the situation, her appearance, her failures; although more so her life in general.

Daisy pulled herself up off the floor and tore the latest ensemble from her sweaty body. She wiped her face roughly and dug under the clothes for her dressing gown. She threw it on and tied it, slightly too tight, so loosened it again. She was so angry at herself. *How could she have allowed herself to become such a state?* She used to be so 'together', so 'organised'. If nothing else she had at least had her emotions in check most of the time. She let out a huge sigh and diverted her gaze from the mocking mirror. Coffee. She needed coffee.

Just as she was heading down the stairs looking and sounding like a stroppy teenager the house phone started to ring. She cursed under her breath but sped up her pace. Seven rings and it would stop. There was not much she hated in the world, usually, but the person hanging up just as you reached the phone was one of them.

"Hi Sweety, how are you?" her Mum's ever chirpy voice rang out down the line.

"Oh, hi Mum, yea I'm alright, just packing for tomorrow."

"Excellent, I've just finished mine. I was ringing to see if there was anything you wanted me to bring, or pick up on the way over."

"Erm, no, I don't think so. I had the shopping delivered today so there should be plenty in for you and kids."

"That was very kind, but we could have done a little bit of shopping while you were away. Well you sound quite stressed so I will let you get on, if you think of anything just send me one of those text message things rather than worrying about ringing. I'll probably be in the garden; it is a lovely day outside."

Daisy envied her mother's love of horticulture. Technically she should have inherited the 'green fingers' that all her family but her seemed to have, she wondered if it might be something that appeared later in life. Maybe once the struggle of keeping a house under control became a natural habit or the children moved out thus, the house was not constantly destroyed.

Right! Decision made, she would go and collect the children from school and then finish her packing. She was no longer in any way in the mood to sort through her clothes. Possibly doing the school walk would burn a couple of extra pounds. Who was she kidding, she knew that she was going to this reunion in a state of desperation and with an exhausted-haven't-bothered-to-exercise-in-years kind of body. *Bugger it.* She muttered to herself as she put on her hoody, jeans and trainers. *Even though I don't have a fabulous body I have the shoes that might assist me in achieving it.* Daisy stood up straight, gave her reflection a smug look and sprinted out of the house.

Chapter One- Being A Grown Up

Daisy smirked to herself as the train sped up; today she was finally stepping out into the world of adulthood, brave, confident and obviously in control of her own destiny. She hoped she was managing to look the part, to blend in with the other grown-ups, but her stomach was not agreeing with her current cognitive process, her stomach was in knots, unsettled to be venturing so far from home, alone. But, as the song went, London was calling.

So here she was, strong and in control. Destiny was in the guise of a school reunion with many people whom she had not missed during the past twenty years. According to the sparkly green and purple invitation, their old school colours, they 'had missed her', and apparently, 'could not wait to see her again'.

The months which had passed too quickly since her invite arrived had been spent mulling over whether or not to attend; *should I, yes, no, maybe, God no.* Yet here she was, heading for Liverpool Street and hoping like hell she had got on the right train. Figuring that if she had, at least she would get a couple of hours without the children, school runs, housework and general impeding boredom. In her mind Daisy ran through the differing potential scenarios of her journey, arrival and event, none of which she hoped would happen. These were the thoughts which had kept her awake on and off all night and the reason her eyes were so puffy, even after a double coating of eye revival serum.

What if she was on the wrong train? What if the train was full of scary, smelly people? What if she had the date wrong? Her stomach gave another lurch. *What if that 'hated foursome' from school were at the reunion and were still hateful and venomous?* Worse still were the immediate thoughts of home, bearing in mind she had only left there half an hour ago. *What if her Mum overslept and Cory missed his exam? Well spelling test, he was only five. What if her Mum forgot to make their lunches and to feed the dog, goldfish and to water the plants?* Ok, plant. The one sad surviving cheese plant which had so far miraculously made it two years, even without Mozart or plant food, or in fact water. But today it was of the upmost importance.

Also, Sally had her 'show & tell'; would they remember or would Sally have to embarrassingly dig deep in the box of 'special' items which the teacher kept for the children of disorganised parents? Sally and Cory had both had occasions to have to do this but today she needed (so as to ease her mother guilt) to know that everything at home was under control and organised. Why it mattered today she didn't know as they had muddled through so far, and Children's Services had not been called in just because her children occasionally smelled of Febreeze rather than fabric conditioner, or because she forgot their PE kits. Or because it was World Book Day and that a crown made from the purposefully finished Cocopops box did not make her daughter the little princess, and a frozen pea and a confused, sleepless night did not mean she was from a Fairytale.

'I'm ok. I'm ok. I'm ok.' She chanted inside her head as the bile rose in her throat. She looked out the window in order to avoid a sudden rush through the now crowded carriage, and into the toilet she had no wish to utilise. To pass the time and to take her mind off her disastrous premonitions, she surveyed her fellow passengers through her long fringe, trying to guess where they were headed and why. The man to her left was 'suited and booted' and obviously important to some company or another. He looked tired and thoroughly bored with his chosen life course. An outward lack of fulfilment? A bad choice which he had deemed a good one back in the day, possibly? Maybe he

was just as tired and as concerned about his home life as she was about hers.

The scenery rushed by, she could make out the newly growing crops, the tractors, already busy working on the fields, the dotted houses, and the healthy looking trees. She loved this time of year as the world was becoming colourful once more. It gave her hope somehow, she was unsure why, but just the fact that they were now waking up to sunshine, rather than eating breakfast and feeling as though it was still the middle of the night, helped lift her mood.

The man two rows to her left was younger than the other man and possibly younger than her, yet, he was also dressed in a grey suit and had the same solemn look in his eyes. Maybe five years ago he was the young sparky, new associate, hoping for big things in the city. From the look of him, he had achieved the large bank balance but not much else, except tired and dull skin and the look of bewilderment almost, at how things hadn't quite turned out as expected. *Isn't that the way*, she thought. 'Unexpected' was a reoccurring word in her life's narrative. A toy dinosaur in the toilet–well that was unexpected. A sickly child throwing up in her bed–well that was unexpected. Her ever expanding reflection in the mirror-well that was unexpected. Matching socks for every pair of feet in the house on a Friday morning-that was definitely unexpected, if not miraculous. Her husband (now ex-husband) of ten years to be found taking regular visits to the public toilets and seedy bars, mostly frequented by a 'certain' type of man. That had most definitely been an unexpected turn of events.

That might be something which she left out of her greeting speech to her long lost school friends, *'Hi I'm Daisy, my husband preferred men to me but I'm not taking it personally, look at me, I've made it all the way to London. We have two beautiful children, Cory aged five and Sally who's seven. I'm on a career break at the moment while the children are still young. So how has the last twenty years been for you?'* Daisy imagined the look on people's faces and smirked.

A young man with funky braces and tie was sat just up the carriage and had the look which she figured the other men had once had, the expectation, drive, ambition… hope. He had yet to succumb to the charcoal grey suit 'can't be bothered to think before I dress' brigade which frequented the inner London trains.

More buildings were being built on the ever-expanding outskirts of Cambridge. If they weren't careful, there would be nothing but a border and signpost separating Cambridge and London in the next few years.

A young lady entered the carriage. A sweet smelling perfume accompanied her and the bored men shuffled higher in their seats, probably in order to be noticed by her. Daisy shuffled down in her seat, trying not to be within comparable distance of this twenty-something girl who looked as though she was in her prime, had found her path perhaps, maybe business or love or children or all of the above. She most certainly looked content and was pulling off the 'grown up' look incredibly successfully.

Daisy enjoyed people watching, it bemused her as to the decisions others had made and the life they were living because of it. She could sit for hours listening to stories of strangers' lives and the choices they had made and how they had panned out for them. Her favourite question was- are they happy? Perhaps this mattered to her because she had yet to find what she classified as happy. The old ladies and gentlemen in the home up the road from her house, where she helped out two mornings a week, regaled elaborate stories of lost love and nights dancing under the stars. Lucid or not, Daisy didn't care, she loved it. She would perch on the seat next to them, her eyes as wide and excited as a child with their Grandparents. The gentlemen, with tears in their eyes, spoke of deceased wives; and the ladies spoke of evenings grouped on the steps of the village hall drinking pop through straws from glass bottles, while they danced the night away with their loved ones, forgetting the poverty or tiredness which beheld their families of that era.

Daisy knew she was looking for answers; the magic ingredient which she had obviously missed while mixing her recipe for a happy life. Her hope may have subconsciously been to one day be let in on the secret and to have a 'eureka' moment- thus resulting in eternal happiness.

Now halfway to her destination she saw the countryside had turned to denser residential areas dotted between fields. The roads were busier, houses were bigger and people were now up and about and getting ready for work or school or settling in for morning TV, in order to be informed of the goings on in the world outside their living room windows, without them having to experience it first-hand. Bearing in mind the way most days turned out maybe the latter was preferable.

The scattered blossom trees were beautiful and once again took her mind back to a time she'd wished to return to ever since it happened and travel to long before it did; the birth of their children. They both… The train jolted, she tried to hide her alarm, cool, calm, collected, grown up… had been born days apart in date in the beginning of June. Blossom trees brought back the joy, the overwhelming love; and these moments and those children would forever tie her and Joel together, no matter what the details of their differing paths.

Daisy believed you could tell a lot about a person and their heritage by their name. Daisy was from a middle class background but her mother had a wild streak, which made her wish to have attended festivals and visit Stonehenge; back in the days when you could actually touch it and you didn't get a guided tour on your mp3. However, she informed Daisy's father that it was her love of flowers which led her to this naming of their child; Daisy loved this fact. Joel, on the other hand, was the son of an extremely manly father, who had worked in construction his whole life and believed a man deserved a loving wife, a meal on the table and every woman deserved a man like him.

Daisy inwardly smiled at the memory of Joel informing his father, with her present (yes she was that supportive), of his new 'situation' concerning his sexual orientation. His mother became slightly hysterical and downed a very large brandy. To this day this was one of Daisy's favourite memories; as to her it was the slap in the proverbial face of Joel's father and all his manly demands and expectations. His father however had held strong, cleared his throat and looked pleadingly at his wife for an appropriate answer; Maude's head was still in the drinks cabinet, stifling her laughter, so he had aimed his look at Daisy, who suddenly saw a very interesting bird land on the birdtable in the rose garden beyond the window, thus avoiding the tension in the room.

Beyond the window of the train, the sheep in the fields looked content that the grass was now green, yet they were a darker shade of white than back at home due to the pollutants nearer to London. The barges on the river gave a smidgeon of bright colours to the greenery and Daisy imagined how relaxing a river holiday with the kids might be. Instantaneously overriding these fantasy-filled thoughts was the realisation that not only was she terrified of travelling alone today but also her fear of water might be a slight hiccup in her master plan and inevitably impact the overall enjoyment of the hypothetical holiday.

The residential areas were now becoming overcrowded council estates and flats; man-made play areas constructed on fake grass consequently leading to seemingly replica childhoods. Everything seemed like an act these days and thus Daisy sunk further in her seat away from the grown-up beautiful people. The similarities of the residents here and in Daisy's life, and her off-spring's childhood, was immense; here, their clothes were hung on balconies with the same love and care as back home. People worked on their allotments in the same way people tended to their gardens and farms in Daisy's village, if not with even more appreciation and consideration. It was barely eight o'clock and yet there they were, this made Daisy not only consider how lucky she was but also saved her sympathising with their lack of space and fresh air, as they obviously saw the same deliberation as everybody else in growing their own veggies and not using the tumble dryer when it's twenty-three degrees outside.

At the sight of the graffiti and withered balloon in the hedgerow, the announcement for 'London, Liverpool Street' rang out. Now she was nervous. She had not physically moved an inch other than to unlock her knees which kept seizing up every few miles, yet the distance she had travelled geographically was immense. She just needed to make it the last half mile once she arrived in order to get to the pre-booked hotel.

Out of the window there were more barges on the river and cyclists, and a pub with a sign reading, something '…and Hope'. She had once had her Angel cards read on a rare girl's night out at Sam's house. They had informed her that she should 'read the signs', 'hope', she now needed a sign reading 'you'll be ok'. She spotted the phallic looking building marking the millennium. God what was that called again? The melon? The egg? Ah she had no idea. She'd Google it later. It looked out of place amongst the high-rise flats. They paused at another station, 'London Fields' that was irony at its best, and a past history only remembered by Wikipedia researchers.

She smirked with excitement and intrigue upon seeing the huge concrete structures and considered the graffiti to be the flowers of the city. She was in London baby! She wanted to jump up and dance and visit the 'Las Vegas Airbrush tattoo parlour' and get it tattooed on her arm, to prove she was really here.

Chapter Two- London Baby!

The smell of London collided with her nostrils as she stepped off the platform. It was an indescribable one consisting of fumes from the many trains, sweat from fellow passengers and perfumes and just London. The sensation instantly comforted her and reminded her of childhood trips to grandparents' houses. She had an urge to grab a train to Richmond and go run in the park and climb trees. Emotion threatened to overwhelm her. So, she stood straighter and headed through the crowds with a purposeful look, her mantra playing through her head, 'look like you know where you are going'. She resisted double checking the directions on her hand and instead read the signs and looked, hopefully, decisive.

Walking up the stairs of the Broadgate exit Daisy felt as though they were being set free into a higher world as the sun illuminated the people above her and finally found her. Confidence and excitement replaced her previous fear and she smiled. She felt strangely safe and unusually strong. After all the concerns she had had at this moment she knew the decision to come had been the right one.

Walking down Broadgate Street she breathed deep and observed the shiny exteriors of the differing building and then dared to glance at her reflection- she looked- youthful and aspiring- dare she look again- *what if she saw different?* She felt the stresses and strains of the past few years being left behind.

Her phone chimed, a text from her mum, all in capitals, as she was unable to change the settings and had probably taken half an hour to write- KIDS AT SCHOOL X. Daisy smiled. She knew her mum would now be making a lovely cup of sweet tea in the one cup and saucer set remaining from their wedding set. Then the rubber gloves would be on and she would be on a mission to spruce the house, even though Daisy had practically ripped the house apart and scrubbed it within an inch of its life. Her mum would still find the invisible dirt which would obviously have appeared overnight. This was not a malicious move on the part of her mother, so much as a show of genuine affection. A mother's love, a gift to Daisy for all her hard work.

The organisation skills which Daisy herself had not inherited, would mean the kids would have put dirty washing away, washed up after breakfast and probably even brushed their hair and teeth rather than choosing between the two. Her mum would have provided them with an amazing lunch unlike the regular one Daisy sent them off with, even though the food in the cupboards was the same. This did not bother Daisy in the way it might other daughters, she admired it and hoped the mother gene would kick in sometime before the kids finished university.

Daisy made her way to the hotel where the reunion was to take place; she had pre-booked as soon as she had decided to attend, before she changed her mind again. She always followed through with plans once she had agreed to them, thus removing the option of opting out. Experience had taught her that her first instinct was usually the right one and that the doubting of said decision was based on pure fear. She reminisced about the many shopping trips where she had ended up back in the first place she had spotted something.

The hotel was easy to locate via the smudged directions scribbled on the back of her hand. That would teach her to use too much antibacterial spray; good old 'risk society' which had created a world filled with fears and concerns every step of the way. No matter how much Daisy logically knew that the buying of antibacterial spray was not going to stop her contracting some icky disease, she welcomed the concept that it may possibly prevent it. The fact that she understood that as a consumer she was being fed these media concerns and panics and thus she was compelled to buy more products in order to alleviate the risk, as best she could.

The receptionist was a friendly lady, ready to help and understanding that the many travellers in their establishment had travelled far and possibly unsure of their surrounding thus needing reassurance. If this had been in the job description then they had picked the perfect person for the job. Jan, as her name badge read, greeted Daisy with a smile and efficiently passed her the key card and simultaneously summoned the porter, with smile of a saint. Daisy was almost scooped up and deposited in her room before she could catch her breath.

Her room was stunning and Daisy felt instantly tired seeing the comfy bed and well presented with a choice of a soft or hard pillow clearly labelled. She tipped the porter and kicked off her shoes. The carpet was so soft that her toes involuntarily started snuggling themselves into the carpet. She climbed onto the bed and just lay still for a few moments with a huge grin on her face. All anxieties aside, she was content in this instant, if not just a tad proud of herself for having successfully tackled this adventure alone. Yet as quick as it had overwhelmed her it passed and back came her all too familiar mother-guilt. She reached for the phone which elegantly sat on the nightstand and rang her mum, to let her know that she had arrived safely. Her mum praised her for getting there in one piece and followed up with an enquiry as to where all the cleaning products were kept.

"Under the sink, as you know."

"I know that, but you've run out."

Daisy rarely ventured into this area of her kitchen but although she had spritzed the house yesterday, she was in no way running low on anything. She had barely been left the house three hours and her mum had already used everything up- wow! She was extremely excited by the prospect of how clean her house would be. However, as she lay in the cream and mocha room, she did not allow herself to think too much of home. Instead she directed her mum to the local shop and the porcelain chicken which should have held eggs but instead kept loose change and general odds and sods. Her mum brushed off the offer of change and informed her that she had no oven cleaner left, *hmm*, though Daisy she couldn't actually remember the last time she'd bought any let alone used it. But who was she to stop her mother from doing what she enjoyed, she was most certainly not about to complain about the imminent cleaning.

Daisy languidly stretched from her fingers right down to her toes, then lazily reached to check the time on her phone. Nearly 8pm, *Lord!* She must have just zonked. It had been a deep sleep, all the nervous energy of the trip and the apprehension about tomorrow's reunion had caught up with her.

She hastily rang reception to check whether she was too late for dinner, apparently not. Fantastic. She popped into the ensuite to freshen up. Daisy surveyed her reflection, it was always strange to view yourself in a different mirror, like bumping into someone who you recognise but can't place because they are out of the regular surroundings in which your encounter them. She shook the thought off and got her bag together. She couldn't be bothered to change; to be honest, although the hotel was lovely it was not necessarily the kind of establishment where you had to 'dress' for dinner. She'd hopefully be ok in her comfy jeans and slobby jumper slung over her tatty travelling t-shirt. She understood after studying many magazines that jeans were not an especially flattering look for her size 14 figure but seriously, who was looking? She was comfy.

Scuttling past the reception desk, the friendly receptionist had changed to a slightly less friendly looking lady, who did not look best pleased to be working an evening shift. She attempted a civil smile.

"Evening," she greeted, more through habit than genuine acknowledgement.

Daisy considered that there might be a censor which triggered her to greet guests as they entered the zone.

The concierge directed Daisy to a 'table for one', which was practically central to the room, as though she was the entertainment and at any moment a spot light would hit her and she may start singing and dancing on her table, which was practically the size of a tray. Daisy not being overly comfortable in public places (or home) at the best of times found this incredibly terrifying. As ever in these moments of discomfort Daisy was getting anxious; then she started to feel slightly flushed and the more anxious she got about being anxious the symptoms became worse. Luckily they provided napkins and Daisy endeavoured to mop her brow as discreetly as possible. Not an easy feat given her location.

Her waiter, thankfully, arrived to take her order, the menu of which she hadn't even glanced at yet, other than to use it as a shield against the growing interest of the other diners. There was only a handful of people, most of whom seemed to have finished their meals and were relishing in each other's company. *Well good for them.* Daisy thought, marginally spitefully.

"Lasagne, please, with salad and a glass of dry white wine, thank you." Daisy used such an order as her 'safe bet' the majority of establishments served lasagne and she never frequented the kinds of places in which the chef would be offended at such a request. Luckily for Daisy her 'safe bet' paid off.

"Certainly, Mam," replied the young waiter while retrieving the unread menu from her grip.

From relief at her order being accepted Daisy allowed the 'Mam' to pass and smiled. What the bloody hell was that? How old did she look? Perhaps he was viewing her from her creased-from-the-pillow side. Perhaps she was just looking old, and worse still alone.

As another flush took over her, the feeling of which was now intensified, she could feel the room start to spin. *Pull yourself together* she instructed herself. It was working, she was beginning to breath normally again, then as if from nowhere the sensation of vomit overwhelmed her and she rose sharply from her chair, the vase with a single fake red rose ended up taking up residence on the floor.

In reflection, once safely back in her room, Daisy wondered if she could have handled it differently. *Yes, most definitely, you should have stayed at home!* Her earlier elation has dissipated and the urge to cry had replaced the urge to throw up. She sat on the edge of the bed, feeling pure mortification at her pathetic attempt at dining out alone. She had read that it was considered empowering to deliberately treat yourself to a lovely meal out, enjoying the atmosphere and the pure indulgence of it all. *Erm, no,* interrupted her inner voice. She had struggled to attend the gym alone and that was a pursuit for fun that was more of a compulsion; to attain once more her major muscle groups, to be able to accomplish stairs without passing out but her primary objective, to rediscover her stomach muscles. The verdict after a year of slogging her guts out was still out in whether they had removed them during her children's births. So far it was leaning towards the latter.

A knock at the door broke her moment of self-pity.

"Mam, I brought you your lasagne."

Daisy smiled wide and gratefully at the young waiter who had obviously observed her display but bless him, he had no idea that he had been the straw that broke the camel's back, so to speak. Him and his 'Mam'.

Chapter Three- Hotel Insomniacs

After a disturbed night's sleep where she swapped hourly between the soft and hard pillows and had somehow managed to wrap herself in knots in the duvet. Daisy awoke feeling as though she had run a marathon. She laid still for a moment to catch her breath from the exertion. Long gone were the days where she had woken up feeling this exhausted for a reason involving not much sleep and an athletic man. She blushed at the thought and simultaneously felt down at the realisation that those days were well and truly a part of her historic legacy, rather than anything which could be something to look forward to. It was these kinds of moments that made her feel much older than her 36 years. According to statistics she should be in her sexual prime. This she considered might be true, however without a willing male participant it would be hard to prove.

She swung her legs out of the bed and padded to the bathroom. Catching a glimpse of her reflection the realisation of why there was no willing man was confirmed. She looked old, tired and deflated, and not just in the airless-balloon-of-her-muscle-tone kind of way, but in a life-had-taken-its-toll kind of way. No amount of diet, exercise and pampering was going to return her youth to her lagging image. She sat on the toilet, contemplating her options in life. Her decision was made. She would do as she always had. Keep her head down and look after her family to the best of her ability and fly under the radar in terms of love interest. She didn't have any more to give and the miniscule amount of get up and go she had retained after the divorce settlement was needed for her children. She cleaned her teeth and splashed her face with water and left the bathroom mirror to criticise the tile choices rather than her.

Daisy was in two minds whether to head downstairs for breakfast or to go and explore London for a few hours before she needed to get ready for tonight's reunion. She was apprehensive about embarking on either; especially after last night's disastrous episode. However, she needed to get brave, how could she walk into the reunion later if she couldn't even master the art of eating alone? She popped on a 'make-do' outfit and made her way to the lift, her mantra of the day running through her head, *I can do this, I can do this*. Had she not have been in a public place she probably would have argued back, she did not feel at all as though she 'could do this'. Quite the opposite in fact. But she had spent most of her life plastering on a smile and pretending to be confident so she would carry on with the façade which had fooled many a person before.

"Morning," chimed Jan, the friendly receptionist from yesterday as Daisy skulked across the foyer, only one step away from hiding behind the randomly placed shrubs, in order to covertly eat and leave. Instead true to form she smiled and returned the greeting.

"Morning."

"Did you sleep ok?" Jan continued.

Daisy took the opportunity to befriend someone for a moment. She wandered over and leant against the reception desk, "To be fair, no, not really, I was too on edge."

Jan pulled a sympathetic face, "Oh bless your heart, was it just because you were in a strange place?"

"Yes most probably and it's hard being away from my children, I rarely leave them."

"Well that's understandable. Have you travelled far?" she genuinely seemed interested.

"From Norfolk, so a fair way I guess."

"Oh, it's beautiful there, I used to holiday in Sheringham with my grandparents."

"Yes Sheringham is lovely, I take the children there sometimes, and we have family there."

"Oh lucky you, I haven't been there for years. So what are your plans for the day?"

Daisy filled her in on her plans to potter around the shops and to relax in the afternoon before stressing over preparing for the reunion. She was so nervous. After twenty years how would she have a clue who people were or what to talk to them about?

"How exciting though? Do you still keep in touch with any of them?"

"No, not really, only via Facebook. I wish I had more contact with some of them, then I could have travelled with them or met up with them beforehand, but hey ho. Worst case scenario is that I escape early and head for home."

Daisy had already learned how to emergency call her mobile. Best to be prepared in these scenarios.

"Oh, I'm sure it won't come to that, once you get there and you catch up with a few of the ones you remember you won't want to leave." Jan beamed at her, inspiring her to relax a bit about it all. She hadn't considered that she might enjoy herself; always the pessimist.

Daisy bided Jan farewell and headed for the dining area, it was much busier than last night and with her newly acquired optimism, she viewed the other guests as far friendlier and less threatening. She decided not to try to spot anyone who might have witnessed her display; instead, she strode confidently across to the tray stand and then made a B-line for the coffee and toast.

She seated herself at a table tucked away by the window, the view was nothing of much interest, just concrete and traffic but then she was in London and it was still nice to watch the world go by. At home there was hardly any through traffic but stunning views. It was relaxing to watch people coming and going, people watching was one of her favourite pass times. She made little stories up in her mind of who they were and where they were going and why. It passed the time and occupied her troubled mind. She was looking forward to chatting to the children after breakfast as she had given them time to chill out with Nanny before talking to her; she did not want to be too over protective.

Her mum was more than capable of looking after the children and she wanted them all to enjoy their time together. She did, however, miss them terribly. Part of her did not want to consider the fact that life was ticking over quite nicely back home without her in it. *Hmm.* Maybe a selfish mother part of her wanted them to miss her. To get the phone call of 'Mummy please come home we miss you so much'. Daisy was aware that she was almost wishing for an escape route and that phone call would be just the excuse she needed to return home and forget about this ridiculous reunion.

"Excuse me, do you mind if I join you?" Daisy was jolted out of her thoughts.

"No not at all, please do," replied Daisy to the nervous plump woman as she smiled kindly down at her; gripping her tray as though it was a life raft.

"Thank you. Sorry to disturb you, there seemed nowhere else to sit."

"Honestly it is fine, I felt bad taking up a four-seater anyway so you have relieved me of that guilt."

The lady giggled. Daisy observed her for a moment. She was about ten years older than her, she wore a wedding ring which looked as though it had been placed on her finger long before she had acquired the extra few pounds. She was biting her lip in a worried way and she had chosen an espresso, a sign of another fellow hotel insomniac. Her clothing was similarly chosen as Daisy's, in that it was for comfort rather than style.

"I'm Daisy by the way." She gave a smile and a little wave.

"Hello, I'm Georgie," she smiled wide, also pleased to have someone speak to her.

A few moments passed as they sipped their coffee and nibbled at their breakfasts. The street was slowing its pace. Obviously, the workers were now firmly placed at their respective destinations. The people who were filling the pavements now were seemingly there for recreational purposes. Maybe that was what she needed, some window-shopping, and possibly a small amount of retail therapy. Maybe she should go and purchase a book and find a quiet coffee shop. She could doze while appearing to read... tempting.

Georgie spoke, breaking Daisy out of her daydream. "So may I ask what brings you here? Sorry, whatever I said it would sound like a bad chat-up line." She giggled, making Daisy smile widely.

"I'm here for a school reunion," she replied, holding back the urge to grimace. "How about you?"

"Oh how exciting, how many years since you all meet up? Me? I'm visiting my daughter and her family." Georgie seemed as equally enthralled by her situation.

"Twenty years, it seriously doesn't seem possible. Does your daughter live nearby then?" Daisy preferred these double conversations, it saved her having to spill the beans about her own sad life and reasons for being here alone. Georgie appeared to be keeping up quite well, there was obviously much more detail she would like to add to the controversial conversation. Yet she was keeping it light for now.

"I know the years fly by don't they?" she added wistfully, then with a more serious tone, "Casey, her husband and daughter live about a mile away… they don't have space for me to stay with them. And they are very busy." She added almost knowing the next question that would be posed.

A sadness passed over Georgie's eyes so Daisy tactfully avoided more questioning along this line, it was obviously a sensitive subject.

"So do you have children?"

"Yes, two, and at this moment I have immense mother guilt as I have left them in the loving care of my mother."

"Oh we all have that, my dear, no matter how old they get I'm afraid. So when is your reunion?"

"Tonight." Daisy let out a deep nervous sigh.

"Fabulous, do you have a stunning outfit all ready?"

"Well, I have an outfit, but I'm not sure the word stunning would be one I would use," Daisy laughed, "I'm a tad old to be stunning."

Georgie looked her straight in the eyes, the older lady stated, "You are stunning, and by no means old, if you don't mind me saying so. What I wouldn't give to only be twenty years out of school." Her kind eyes showed a twinge of regret and sadness behind her smiling face. Daisy wanted nothing more than to give her a hug. She appeared to be holding one tight to the emotion that was threatening to overwhelm her. A hug might break the façade and lead to an emotional torrent. She wondered why it was that kind words from a stranger seemingly held more truth in them than those from loved ones. Honesty, might be a better way to explain it, Daisy considered, they weren't just trying to please you, they are seeing each other for who they were at that exact moment, without judgement. Daisy cleared her throat, aiming to remove the lump which had taken up residence there.

She took a sip of coffee and picked at the remands of her toast. Both women looked out of the window.

"I enjoy imagining what kind of day each person is having or where they are going. Silly really." Georgie almost apologised for her comment.

Daisy turned to look at her, "Me too."

That was it; Daisy had found a likeminded person.

Georgie and Daisy sat chatting and discussing every viable subject known to man. They enjoyed being able to relax and get to know someone new. Daisy loved hearing about other people's lives, how they had reached this point in life, how the decisions they had made along the way had shaped them into the person they were now. She also found it hugely therapeutic to talk about her own life. It was moments like this that Daisy truly believed that people met for a reason, good or bad. They were deep in conversation when a waitress approached them, breaking them out of their conversational bubble.

"Would you like to see the lunch menu?"

Both women looked back at each other and burst out laughing. Had they seriously been here for three hours?

"Erm, no thank you, I really must go," replied Daisy. She instinctively scooped up her cardigan and handbag. She understood that the young lady was being tactfully polite in asking this and wanted them to leave. In all fairness, Daisy always thought people were just tactfully polite to her and wished she would just leave. Something else to put on her ever expanding to-do-list, *change mental attitude towards oneself*. It was time to start realising that sometimes people really did like her and want to spend time with her; it was not always out of sheer obligation.

"Are you busy Georgie? Do you fancy a wander around the shops with me?" Daisy felt this was a brave move and if the answer was no she would fully understand. She vowed not to burst into tears once back in her room. She realised she was holding her breath, bracing herself for the response.

Georgie looked up from where she was retrieving her bag and looked almost startled and confused. Then a wide smile stretched across her face and a slight blush flushed her cheeks.

"Very much so. I mean, I would love to come with you," she stammered, "if you don't mind. I don't need to be at my daughter's until teatime."

With huge relief, Daisy matched her smile and they made their way out of the dining area. They agreed to meet back in the lobby in half an hour. This gave them both time to brace themselves ready for exploring London. For Daisy it gave her time to ring her mum and check all was well at home. Jan acknowledged them both as they passed her desk, with a knowing smile that the two women had befriended each other.

Chapter Four- Ladies Who Lunch

The children were both fine and apparently far too busy, and messy, to come to the phone. According to her mum they had slept well and they were all now enjoying baking cookies, fairy cakes and jam tarts. Daisy smiled as her mum regaled the events of the past twenty-four hours. She was so pleased that they were all enjoying themselves; however, she felt a stab of jealousy at not being a part of it. *Yes,* she confirmed to herself, *you do need to learn to loosen the apron strings*. Daisy was fully aware that since Joel had left that she overprotected the children and overcompensated for the lack of a fatherly presence in their home. The innate tigress in her knew that with the father being away from the cubs meant that they were more vulnerable, but then the wrath of a tigress protecting her young was one of pure force... one not to be messed with! Daisy sent huge mummy hugs to the children via her mum and thanked her for watching them for her. As ever, her mum reassured her that it was her pleasure and Daisy knew she meant it, she loved her grandchildren profusely.

Daisy had a quick shower, keeping her hair out of the way of the stream of water; she really didn't have time to contend with that. Dressed in her comfy jeans and thin black jumper, she applied a swift swipe of make-up, a straightening of her fringe, she grabbed her cardigan, handbag and slipped on her black pumps.

Georgie stood up from the purple tub chair as Daisy exited the lift. They were both excited to be spending the day in good company and in a wonderfully exciting city. They nattered away like school girls as they strode down the street, hardly noticing the shops as they were so engrossed in their conversation. Georgie was recalling her many trips to London over the past five years that her daughter had lived there. She, personally, lived in a little place just outside, Lincoln, called

Bracebridge Heath. Although it too was a city, Georgie explained that it was a rural city so quite a contrast to London. She told Daisy of the many days which she had spent trawling the streets just aimlessly waiting for her daughter to ring her to come over, once they had finished work for the day. Georgie's eyes filled up at the loneliness she had felt as she had travelled so far to visit a family who seemed as though they had no appreciation for her. Daisy found this difficult as from the few hours in which she had known Georgie she seemed a lovely lady.

Daisy understood that every family had issues and things that were not necessarily on the surface at first glance into a person's life. However, she was not about to make assumptions about the daughter who was neglecting a loving mother, as every story has two very different sides. Daisy just listened to this lady pour her heart out and hoped that the reactions she was giving where the right ones without criticism or commitment. Many questions popped in to Daisy's mind but she in no way knew this woman well enough to ask any of them. Perhaps she would mentally pop them to one side in case she ever did meet her again. Daisy had to admit that she felt as though Georgie was in fact an old friend who she was reconnecting with after years apart. She felt strangely comfortable in her company. This was exactly what Daisy had needed a nice day of chilling out and chatting. Georgie also appeared to be thoroughly enjoying herself.

Mid-sentence about her family Georgie suddenly stopped in front of a shop window, "Wow those shoes are amazing… shall we go in?" She turned with wide childlike eyes.

Daisy laughed out loud at her new friend. "Definitely!

Smiling widely the two of them entered the shop, their eyes lit up at the wide variety of shoes all placed elegantly on mirrored shelves under their own mini spotlights. They were like kids in a sweetshop, practically drooling over the beautiful candy. Georgie just stood staring at the diamanté covered stilettos. Daisy was standing in awe at a pair of purple flowered boots.

"Can I help you," asked a well-spoken lady. Both women physically jumped as the voice broke through their daydreams. They simultaneously turned to face her.

"Would you like to try them on ladies?"

They both turned to each other for conformation.

"Erm," They shrugged their shoulders.

"What size are you both?" She surveyed their feet as she asked. She aimed her gaze at Daisy, "Size 6?" and then at Georgie, "Size 5?"

They both just nodded, their mouths still gapping both at her presence and at her skill of knowing their shoe sizes just by looking at their feet. The lady glided away silently. Daisy and Georgie looked around for a place to perch. On finding some comfy stools with foot rests they placed their bags to the side of them.

Daisy leaned towards Georgie conspiratorially, "I hope I have matching socks on," They giggled. Georgie replied, "I hope my feet don't smell."

They were giggling away when the lady returned with two white shoe boxes. She smiled at them, obviously having regularly observed this kind of behaviour, as she removed the lids and moved the tissue paper to one side. The lady took the shoes out, presenting them to Georgie as though they were the crown jewels. For all intent and purposes they may as well have been. She slipped it effortlessly onto Georgie's tight laden foot. Georgie looked nervous to try and stand in them through fear of breaking them, they were so delicate. But as she stood in front of the mirror, lifting her full length skirt slightly higher to get a proper view of the shoes, she twisted and turned. Daisy 'ohed and ahed' at her, the diamanté shimmering as she moved.

"Wow, these are the most beautiful shoes I have ever seen, let alone worn."

Daisy sat with bated breath as the shop assistant unveiled her boots. They slipped on with ease, *this woman was amazing at her job*, thought Daisy, as she stood by Georgie, mimicking her moves in the mirror. The lady waited calmly and unfazed by the stools.

"These boots are stunning… I could live in them."

"They are beautiful."

They playfully showed off their footwear to each other, prancing and laughing together; Daisy with her jeans rolled up to her knees and Georgie holding her skirt and swishing it wildly. The lady smiled along with their shenanigans.

Georgie whispered in Daisy's ear, "How much are these? There is no price on anything."

"That means they are very expensive," Daisy whispered back.

Georgie bit her lip nervously. Daisy made her way back to the stools.

"How were they, ladies?"

"They are the most fabulous shoes ever. Could we ask how much they are please?"

The two new friends made their way back up the street, arms linked through each other's, their hands free of bags. The shoes and boots turned out to be almost a month's income to Daisy, not something she could justify right now, or probably ever. Georgie's credit card was maxed out due to this trip to see her daughter.

"I miss my shoes, please can we go and see them on the way back to the hotel?" begged Georgie.

Daisy laughed out loud. "Only if you behave in the other shops," she jested.

This was turning out to be a wonderful day, Daisy couldn't remember the last time she had laughed, talked or generally enjoyed herself so much, especially with someone she hardly knew. She allowed herself to feel relaxed as they moved from window to window, admiring the differing goods available. They refrained from entering any more shops down this road as they were now fully aware that they could not afford anything that they had to offer. It took a lot of willpower, however, as there were some stunningly displayed items, almost calling out to be bought. To congratulate themselves on their strength of will they sat in the window of 'William's' a quaint little coffee shop tucked just off the main high street and ordered cappuccinos and Danish pastries.

As they unravelled their Danish pastries and picked out the juicy raisins, Georgie questioned Daisy about her fast approaching reunion. Daisy explained about her apprehension at attending and that she had decided spur of the moment and booked the hotel to stop herself changing her mind again. She explained to her it was not so much that she didn't want to see people from school but more the trepidation of what their opinion of her would be. What with the situation being as it was, being a single mum with two children, and a gay ex-husband. Not to mention her lack of career prospects. Just saying these out loud caused a lump in her throat.

She had not got married with the expectation of it not lasting forever. Even more than that, if she had for a second thought that she would become a single mum she would not have borne him two children, no matter how adorable they were. She had grown up, as most young girls do, with the expectation of getting married, buying a beautiful house, white picket fence, and children laughing and playing in the garden as the two of them (her true love and her) sat doting over their idealistic lifestyle and discussing how blessed they were. Instead the bubble had burst at Joel's announcement of gayness… truth be known, Daisy was not in the least bit impressed.

Of late she had felt inwardly angry at the fact that Joel had deceived her with his muscular body and shining smile and promises of forever. Yet at her less harsh moments she understood that he had been trying to live up to the expectations of society but mainly of his parents. She had just been the fallout.

Georgie sat nodding and verbally agreeing as Daisy poured her heart out, she had shocked herself at some of her statements, not having realised she even felt such things. But it felt cathartic to talk to someone who was not involved in the situation and didn't even know Joel; or her for that matter. Yet when Daisy finally got to the real crux of the reason the reunion had caused her so much indecision, Georgie smiled widely and sat back, armed folded and a big knowing smile on her face.

"There you go. Now I understand."

Daisy looked at her with guilt ridden eyes. "Do you think that is wrong of me?"

"Not at all, I think given everything that you have just told me it makes perfect sense."

Daisy's shoulders unwielded themselves from her ear lobes. Finally she had admitted to her true feeling about herself and most importantly her fears. Maybe this talking therapy thing did work because she had talked about it before with friends and family and drawn very different opinions of it all. It had taken a complete stranger listening to her without judgement for this realisation to happen. Probably, Daisy considered, the fact that she was on unfamiliar territory as well had helped. Her normal defences were down and she was not having to pretend to be strong and in control. Also Georgie was extremely open about her own life so it seemed perfectly natural to join in. Daisy felt as though a weight had been lifted. She had faced her demon and it was not as scary as she had thought; although it was still just as ugly as she had imagined it would be.

Chapter Five- Virtual Friends

Daisy returned to the hotel around five having decided not to have dinner tonight. Her outfit for the reunion had only just fitted at home and she was not going to risk it not fitting now. She started the shower and removed her clothing, she needed to wash the smell of London off her, it had made her skin feel greasy and her hair dirty. The feel of the water gently massaging her skin felt relaxing, she had had such a lovely day with Georgie. She almost wished she could have skipped the reunion and spent a quiet evening sipping coffee and chatting, rather than having to be sociable to virtual strangers; although taking into consideration Facebook she guessed they were indeed virtual friends, at best.

Drying herself off Daisy felt deflated. She knew that she should have been excited about meeting up with old friends and having time away from home in order to party in the city but her heart was not in it. Her emotions kept sweeping over her in waves from marginally mardy to pure melancholy. *Snap out of it,* she instructed herself. Nope, that hadn't worked either. She wondered why it was that she never seemed to enjoy the kinds of events that most people apparently thought were fabulously fun. *Was she odd or just more of a 'home-body'?* She perched on the edge of the bed and picked up the receiver to ring home, hopefully speaking to her mum and the children would cheer her up. It was possible, she considered as the tone rang, that she was just still overwhelmed by mother guilt, thus explaining her lack of enthusiasm.

"Mummy!" exclaimed Sally. Daisy's face was instantly covered with a smile and her heart felt lighter. Tears pricked her eyes. If there was one thing in the world she had needed it was that. "Hi Mummy," came Cory's little voice down the line. "We miss you." They chimed. Daisy had an inkling that her mum had instigated this but she didn't care, her children were her world and they missed her and that was all she needed to know. The world could have stopped at that exact second and she would not have batted an eyelid as she was enveloped in her children's love.

"Hi Honey, how is London?" Her mum's voice broke through the children's nattering.

"Good thanks," she managed to say through her tears.

Her mum chatted for a few minutes and the children filled in things she missed out, Daisy laid back against the pillows just listening to them all. She closed her eyes, almost in an attempt to be transported home. She made 'hmms' and 'ahs' as she listened to them regale their trip to the park and how had had to stop Nanny Helena falling in. Daisy could envisage this little scenario in her mind. She grinned at the idea that her children would be holding Nanny back from the duck pond.

Knowing her children Nanny would have been told off by them for not behaving responsibly around the water. She wondered if Sally and Cory had threatened that they would not take her again because she had not behaved properly. Daisy giggled. A pang of love for them and loneliness at being so far away struck her. She was heading for home tomorrow anyway but it seemed such a long time and she still had to face this reunion. She gave a deep sigh.

After hanging up the phone Daisy mentally snapped herself out of her mood. *Right,* she informed herself in her bossy tone, *Let's get ready, stop moping and go and have some well-deserved fun.* She squeezed into her body-transforming underwear and slipped her dress over the top. After fighting with her black firming tights she popped her purple shoes on. Daisy was not a girlie, shoe-loving kind of person, however these shoes broke the barrier. They were truly beautiful shoes that just made her feel more attractive to be near them. Arguably they were by no means as stunning as the boots, but they also had not cost a months' wages. She did love them though, they were three inch heeled, bright purple, suede with gold trims and a dainty bit around the ankle.

Daisy was not impressed by her overall reflection but her feet looked stunning. Her black knee-length dress was very fifties looking with a floaty skirt and a purple belted waist. It looked ok, all the better for the underwear and the general feeling of disregard for where she was going.

She carefully applied her foundation and set to sorting her hair. Firstly, she straightened her long fringe and then the rest of her hair. Once straightened it reached the middle of her shoulder blades. After applying the rest of her make-up she stood in front of the full-length mirror and turned and twizzled just as her and Georgie had done earlier in the day. She was surprised to find that she was actually pleased with her efforts. She looked good, strong, confident and stylish. Well, at least she should not be perceived as complete minger. Hopefully.

Daisy took the lift down to the lobby and followed the sign to the ballroom which had been aptly decorated in green and purple. *At least her shoes would match the colour scheme*, thought Daisy. A desk was set up by the door with two very smiley similarly aged women to Daisy. They asked her name and passed her a premade name badge. Then they started chatting about the old days and how exciting this reunion was. Daisy plastered the smile on her face which she had previously saved for her ex-husband when he had started talking about fishing. Moments later a familiar face appeared, slightly too close, and exclaimed pure joy at seeing her again. Daisy hugged the person back as they pulled her into a friendly embrace. Over Fleur's shoulder she got her bearings of the room and worked out the quickest route to the bar.

A polite time later Daisy bided Fleur a 'see you in a bit' and aimed, undeterred to the bar.

She grabbed for the wooden life raft as though her life depended on it, she had forgotten just how hard it was to walk in these shoes, she was experiencing minor vertigo from them. She decided that she would replace the head-spinning with alcohol inducement. An attractive barman appeared in front of her with a smile that glinted as bright as the glasses he was proffering cocktails in. He expertly mixed her a piña colada and placed an umbrella with a cherry attached to it. Daisy watched in awe as he moved with pure grace. He was exceptionally stunning, Daisy being, felt empathy for him and the drunken women who would almost definitely drool over him. Obviously, Daisy was not that kind of person, however, this seemed like a delightful enough spot she could hide in for the rest of the evening. He smiled at her and asked if the drink was ok. She nodded and wiped her mouth gracefully. Some of her drink must have escaped her mouth.

Daisy turned on her heel and surveyed the room's occupants. As ever at these kinds of events the lighting was low with disco lights flashing up odd parts of the space in a rhythmic way. The music was currently playing in the background so people could mingle. Daisy tried to observe people from over the top of her glass as she sipped her pina colada through a purple and green stripped straw which matched the umbrella. To the far right of the room was a gaggle of slightly pump ladies, all wearing differing versions of floral dresses and flat comfortable shoes. Daisy presumed these were part of the group at school who had hidden in corners not dissimilar to this one. They looked happy to see each other but somehow nervous to be in here. Directly in front of her stood five model-type ladies all of whom were perfectly manicured, slim, blonde and although it was hard to distinguish in this light, slightly orange tinted. Their eyes glanced around them as they addressed each other, in a knowing they were being watched kind of way. Their teeth glowed in the flashing lights as they fake-smiled at each other. It did not take much brainpower to know that these were the same girls who had made all the other girls feel inferior at school and still had the same influence as adults. Daisy felt herself flush as she mentally envisaged how she looked in comparison.

Readjusting her stance she could see a row of men, some tall and thin, others more portly and short. These she figured were the middle of the road kind of blokes. The ones who neither bothered anyone but had just got through the school years having a laugh and bearing average grades. These she remembered were the nice boys, who did not view her with disdain. The same could not be said for the other group of men nearer to the DJ. They were the male equivalent of the beautiful women. These had been the out of reach boys at school. They had been sporty, hugely hyped on hormones and had set the standard of man who Daisy knew she would never land. Her instinct on this had not been far off. As much as Joel had been attractive to her he was more suited to the other group of men; she could lay bets that they would talk fishing with him. She wished things had been different and that Joel could have accompanied her here. For as much as things had turned out different than expected, she missed his air of confidence, especially in these social situations where a strong arm around her would have been welcomed.

She turned away from the quickly filling room, not having realised she had finished her drink until the barman proffered her another one. Daisy felt like one of those sad ladies who stand at the bar all night, drink excessively and end up pouring their hearts out to the nonplussed barman. Ending the night with mascara running down their face and a member of staff has to return them to their room. Maybe if she drunk faster she could speed this process up, and be back in her room within the hour. She could easily start a new Facebook account and block all her old school friends; no one would probably notice she was no longer posting amusing cat pictures on their newsfeeds.

Daisy was so immersed in her plan to escape and the life changes she would have to make afterwards that she didn't realise someone had perched on the barstool next to her. It was not until she heard their voice that her breathing stopped and her knees wobbled more precariously than ever. She had to cling back on to the bar to stop herself falling. This was not a voice she could easily forget. It still had the power to stop her in her tracks. She tried to gain her composure and stood up straighter and sucked her drink with casual togetherness. However, she had also angled her head she they couldn't see her. In reality she knew that with this lighting and after all these years there was little chance of being recognised without introduction to the vast majority of people in here. She could, in fact, be at the wrong reunion and no one would realise. But this one figure next to her made it certain that she was definitely at the right place. Her instinct, as it had been all along, was reaffirmed that yes she wished she hadn't come; she wanted to bolt, book out of her room and go home. Coming here had been a mistake.

Chapter Six- All That Sparkles Is Not Gold

Daisy was removing the cherry from the umbrella in a less that dignified fashion; it appeared to have been welded on.

"Daisy!" Announced a shrill voice, which hushed the entire room. "I would recognise you anywhere. You look stunning. How are you? Is your husband with you?"

Daisy cringed but turned and smiled the fakest friendliest smile she could muster. With one swift glance she read the name tag planted on the left breast of the bubbly lady stood in front of her.

"Verity Richardson. How wonderful to see you." They hugged. Daisy remembered her now, she had always been fairly quiet at school but once you got to know her she had had the most wicked sense of humour. Daisy was genuinely pleased to see her. Although at that exact second as they were exchanging life information, number of children, where they lived, and such, the figure which she had momentarily forgotten was beside her, appeared at her right shoulder.

"So you made it."

"Yes." Daisy replied while Verity had lost her smile and was looking uncomfortable, obviously trying to decide whether to stay or politely back away. She was apparently glued to the spot.

"I didn't think you would come."

"I didn't think you would either."

"Are you well?"

"Yes. You?"

"Very."

"Good."

"Is your husband here?"

"No."

"Is your wife here?"

"I don't have one."

"Oh."

Silence. Awkward cough from Verity. Daisy sipped her near empty cocktail. He stared at her as though he was weighing her up.

"The buffet is open,"announced the DJ. The lights in the room were turned on and everyone squinted for a few moments while their eyes adjusted to the glare. He, however, carried on staring straight at her. Verity finally backed away and smiled reassuringly at Daisy. Daisy emptied her drink.

"How have you been?"

"Good. I've been good."

"For all these years?"

"Yes."

"That's good then."

"Have you been good?" She returned the question.

"At points." *Wow that was honest*, thought Daisy.

"Cool." She had no idea how else to respond to that, any more 'goods' and she might lose it!

While the rest of the room were grazing up and down the buffet, obviously not having eaten dinner either, and were noisily pulling out chairs to sit around tables like civilised people, Daisy just stayed still, now chewing on her straw. It was not so much that she was scared of moving away from his gaze but more that she didn't think her legs would respond if she tried. Thankfully, the barman had slipped her a fresh drink again, she grabbed for it and gave him a grateful smile, he reciprocated. *God he was gorgeous.*

"Well, if it isn't the cutest couple ever. Daisy Green and Tristan Smart. So you two made it the long haul then?" Daisy and Tristan exchanged glances and stared blankly back at, she squinted at the label, Poppy Vermez.

"You are still together, after twenty years. How sweet!" She pulled them both in tight for a group hug. Tristan stood strong and hardly moved, Daisy was flung towards the imposter and with ninja moves saved her drink from sloshing down Poppy's back.

Poppy released them and disappeared as fast as she had arrived off to find some more helpless people. Tristan turned and leant on the bar and Daisy followed suit. These cocktails were going to her head quicker than expected. He pulled a strained face and then turned to Daisy, a questioning look on his face.

"So why didn't we?"

"Why didn't we what?" Daisy was in no fit state for cryptic questions.

"Make the long haul?"

Crap. This was not an anticipated situation, as she had not thought he would bother to come, although secretly she had wished he would. Her mother's voice rang through her ears, *'be careful what you wish for, it might just come true'.* Also, she had not expected him to acknowledge/recognise her, let alone speak to her. Finally, this line of questioning was more personal than Daisy wanted to delve into.

"I don't know." Was all she could slur.

The barman handed Tristan the beer he had ordered and glanced at Daisy, checking she was ok in the company she was in. Daisy wondered whether there were guardian angels and if so, if this barman was hers tonight. Then she wondered how he could conceal his wings and what if they suddenly popped out from under his shirt and broke all the bottles and glasses. *What if…* her line of thought was interrupted by Tristan.

"I don't know either, it has popped into my mind many times over the years and I have never fully worked it out. We were childhood sweethearts, soul mates. We sent letters to each other with S.W.A.L.K. written on the back…"

"Sealed with a loving kiss," she whispered.

"…we loved each other with every cell of our being and here we are stood at this ridiculous event like a couple of strangers."

"Hmm."

The hairs on his forearm brushed hers, just for a moment and Daisy felt a flow of energy pass through her. All the hopes and dreams and stolen moments flashed through her brain, mixed strangely with the angel barman. Emotions threatened to overwhelm her but she somehow managed to compose and excuse herself. She practically ran for the toilet. She was definitely well on her way to tipsy because she had not so much as swayed on her heels, the expert walk of a drunk starting to kick in.

Daisy leant on the worktop which held the three sinks, the gold gilded look was far too portentous to look tasteful. It was like a child had got hold of a gold spray can and decided that gold was their favourite colour, like ever! The soap dispenser, the basket holding the rolled hand towels, the frames of the mirrors, the taps; basically anything that could have been was gold. This mixed with her own reflection was too much. The gold was spinning, her face looked gaunt and sweaty, emphasising her eye make-up, in the wrong kind of way. Instead of bold smoky eyes, she had drag queen eyes. Daisy felt as though her heart had been cut open and Tristan had stuck his whole hand in there, in search of the answers she no longer kept there. Instead they were neatly tucked away in a pretty box, with a ribbon tied around it and labelled 'do not open again'.

The 'again' was the pinnacle word. Daisy reminised about how, years back, in about her late teens, Tristan had contacted her out of the blue and insisted they should meet. By this point she was at college and had had a couple of boyfriends since they had left school, but nothing serious. She decided to be strong and go and meet him. It would be good for them to catch up.

Things had been tense between them since school but they had moved in different circles, so although his name would be heard on the grapevine, they rarely caught a glimpse of each other. Mainly because if Daisy knew he was going to be somewhere she avoided it. If she was shopping and she saw the back of him aiming down an aisle she ran in the opposite direction. Daisy had worked hard to protect herself from the hurt that he caused, well more yearning, in those more honest moments.

So Daisy had spent the day pampering herself, she wanted him to find her attractive and to be amazed by her strength of character and her young independent woman persona. She wanted the smell of her perfume to stay with him longer after she left. She wanted him to wish he had never let her go. She wanted him to proclaim his love for her, sweep her off her feet and wrap his arms around her as he used to do and keep her safe forever. She had wanted him. She had wanted there to be a 'them'.

A cubicle door slammed, breaking her out of her thoughts. She instinctively started washing her hands and readjusting her, now limp looking, hair. The two women exchanged polite toilet sink meeting smiles and continued about their business. The other lady left the toilets and Daisy gave her reflection a stern look, *sort yourself out* she told herself. With that Daisy stood up straight, combed her fingers through her fringe to try to tame the now frizzy appearance of it; readjusted her dress, the belt was digging in and the wedgey caused by these toning tights was possibly permanent. She did the best she could to retrieve them, wherever it was they were aiming, she dreaded to think! *Hey ho* she thought, *at least I can pull off the same look as the tarty women out there and look like I have a stick up my arse, without anyone suspecting that it feels like I have.*

Daisy put on her woman-on-a-mission walk as she excited the toilet. The lights had been turned off again and the disco was in full swing. Daisy smirked as she saw the beautiful women dancing elegantly and the mix-match group of men were still standing as they had been previous to the buffet, just watching. Nothing had changed in all these years. The girls danced and the boys stood awkwardly around the edges of the room. The array of outfits were curious, back at school everyone wore similar styles. The richer kids wore the name branded versions and for ones, such as Daisy, it was a mock up her mum had made her. At the time Daisy had been mortified at wearing handmade clothes, but looking back it was amazing that her mum was so talented, and seriously none of the other children would have known. Tonight, though there were such different personalities, and price ranges, of clothing. Some men wore a full suit, others smart jeans and casual shirt. Some women wore beautiful dresses, other hid in trousers and a semi-glitzy top. You could tell a lot by, not only what people chose to wear, but how they carried themselves while wearing it.

Daisy made her way back towards the bar, walking as straight as was possible. Her hope was to try to relieve some of the pain from her underwear. On approach she realised that Tristan was no longer there. Part of her was relieved and another part disappointed. She tried not to appear obvious in her hunt of him in the room as her eyes darted from one person to another. He was nowhere to be seen. Daisy manoeuvred herself, with very little dignity, up onto a barstool. She swore these were designed to embarrass people, especially once they were drunk, or of a short stature; both of which she currently was.

Once the barman had given her a dignified amount of time to get up on the stool he wandered over.

"You okay?"

"Yes thank you." She answered coolly. It was obvious that she was not.

"Another drink?"

"Yes please but could you do a non-alcoholic version of it?" She gave him a wary smile.

He nipped off and shook lots of differing drinks in his shaker. She endeavoured to not find this in any way rude or erotic. He poured it into a glass with another umbrella and cherry and presented it to her.

"Thank you."

He smiled and then went to serve someone else. Daisy was yet again feeling very alone and although she smiled along with the conversations she had with different people and even had a little dance with Verity at one stage. She was sullen. She managed not to ask after Tristan or overly look for him. Yet part of her wanted to carry on the conversation they had started. As the night passed she found herself relaxing and enjoying herself.

A few of her old 'gang' were there. They had grown up in the same neighbourhood and attended the same primary and secondary schools together. It turned out that Jenson Starr and Chance Laney had started up a business straight out of college in mechanics and they now ran a very successful garage in Twickenham. Nia Morgan was a full-time mum to six beautiful children; the photos in her purse of them were adorable. In all fairness, she had seemed the type to go and become a famous model as she had always been stunning. Although the love in her eyes for her children and husband showed that she was the depiction of the perfect mother and wife. Daisy felt like a proud mother hen whose chicks had grown up and were perfect. She beamed with pride for her friends, who were all grown up.

Chapter Seven- Drunken Daisy

As they all caught up on each other's life events Daisy sipped at her drink. She was now back on the alcoholic version after a short reprieve, she had a pang of regret; no, jealousy. Well whatever the feeling was she didn't like it, she wanted to duck out of the conversation before all eyes turned to her with the dreaded question. It was not to say that everyone else's lives were perfect; it was obvious that they weren't. However, Daisy felt like a failure. Her emotions and life-state were too confusing and raw to fit into a couple of sentences. She worried more that she might cry and as the conversation flowed she felt herself physically shrinking away, hoping no one asked her.

At that moment the music changed, Mel and Kim's 'Respectable' started playing. There were a few whoops and yays. Then Daisy felt her arm being yanked and her drink carefully taken from her hand and placed on the table next to her bag. Debbie pulled her towards the dance floor and as though no time had passed the two of them fell into step with the well-rehearsed routine which they had performed at many a playtime more than twenty-five years ago. Daisy laughed out loud as they effortlessly sang and moved in time. It was the most fun she had had in ages; possibly twenty-five years. *Slight exaggeration.* The rest of the room bopped around the edges and clapped and cheered. Daisy forgot her inhibitions, the cocktails well and truly doing their job. The song finished and the two women hugged and laughed as everyone crowded them as though they were the real Mel and Kim.

She made her way back to the table, flopped down in a chair, just as the barman appeared behind, he leaned over her right side to put a fresh drink on the table.

"Well done," he whispered as he did so.

If Daisy had not been burning up from exertion already she would have appeared to be blushing. Her angel then floated back to his bar, as though his spirit had delivered the drink without him moving. *Yes.* She concluded. *You are a sap. He is just doing his job and looking after the elderly.*

Daisy settled into the flow of the party, she danced and drunk, or was drunk, and laughed and thoroughly enjoyed herself. Her mum had been right when she had conveyed her 'need' for a good night out with old friends. Daisy, at the time, had disagreed although she was also immensely petrified by the idea. If, as ever, she had known that the night would go as well as it did she would have skipped her way merrily to London and around the city that day. But hindsight was an amazing thing. Daisy ruminated over just how many things she would contemplate doing if she knew that everything would turn out well. Then she considered that in that case there would be neither risks nor wonder for the future and ultimately life would be a bore. Daisy loved her drunken thought processes; she was much more fun, open and intelligent when she was drunk.

The evening jollied along with much laughter, and copious amounts of alcohol were served by the seraph barman, who was still regularly taking a second out from his bustling bar to personally top up her drinks. As the night progressed he seemed to have a glowing aura about him too, he was more beautiful than ever. Daisy momentarily paused from the raucous and admired him in all his glory. He was heavenly. She was snapped out of her daydream by a rough push as Nathan Jones fell against her. He apologised profusely as he struggled to stand up straight, laughing loudly and miraculously still holding on to his drink. She forgave him as she understood the turmoil of trying to muster up the expertise they classed as walking. She had not moved from her seat in over an hour due to pure lack of motor skills. She struggled to walk in heels at the best of times let alone after… she had lost count… many cocktails.

As the party came to a close, slow dances had been performed, some with old boyfriends, most by male companions taking the mickey. Daisy had stayed seated, not that anyone had offered. In years gone by she was normally asleep by now, the alcohol having relaxed her, the music lulling and the seat almost swaddled her. It had been after numerous nights out that had ended up as such that Daisy had hung up her clubbing hat; she was safer falling asleep on the sofa at home than on the soiled sofa of a nightclub.

Everyone hugged and bided each other goodbye, vowing not to leave it so long until they did this again. Daisy, even in her intoxicated state, knew that the chances of regular catch-ups were slim, but smiled along and promised to stay in touch. It had turned out to be a fabulous night and she had surprisingly enjoyed reminiscing about her old school days; the teacher they hated, the boys they had fancied, the clothes they had begged their parents for. She was glad she had gone. It had made her forget her worries and feel youthful again. She had managed to steer the conversation away from her disastrous marriage to Joel and talked about her children instead. Preferable to whingeing about her, non-existent career she had claimed to have chosen to be a stay at home mum while the children were young. She had not lied; she had deflected away from the troubling, painful parts of her life. The chances were that everyone else had done the same.

As she stumbled towards the general direction of the door, blowing kisses and feeling tearful at having the party come to an end, a strong arm steadied her. Confused by her sudden stability she turned to see none other than Tristan Smart attached to her elbow. Their eyes meet just for a second and all Daisy could utter was, 'thank you'. She could not hear his reply above the wolf-whistles of her peers. Daisy giggled but was also confused as to where he had been the last few hours and why he was back and, more to the point, why was he holding on to her? Her head hurt just thinking about these things, there was no way her brain was in any fit state to answer them, so she allowed him to carry on holding her. He led her towards the lift and just as they were about to enter it, the barman appeared behind her; she physically jumped at this sudden appearance.

"You forgot your bag," he exclaimed by means of justification for startling her. He looked concerned as he handed her bag over, his eyes bore into her very soul, she wondered if he was upset that she was leaving or just concerned as to who was escorting her. Either way, Daisy was led into the lift away from him and she smiled at him by way of thanks and to assure him that she was perfectly fine. Or she thought she probably could be alright. *What the hell*, she couldn't have cared less. There were worse things that could have happened than being lead to bed by Tristan.

The sunlight steamed through the thin gap between the curtains and bore into Daisy's brain like a laser, *ouch*. She pulled the duvet higher and hid back under it. Her head pounded, ached and generally felt as though she had done a few rounds in the ring with Barry McGuigan; that would teach her to fight outside her weight bracket; she was no featherweight that was for sure. As she lay deathly still hoping the world would stop spinning quite so fast the piecing ring of the bedside phone pierced her sensitive ears through the 13 tog duvet. Somehow, she managed to reach for it without emerging from her cocoon.

"Hello?" she managed in a croaky voice.

"Hello dear, how was the party?" The cheerful tones of her mother sang out, "The children send their love and are most excited that you are coming home today, I think they have missed you." She added in a stage whisper. Daisy could hear that her mum was smiling at the children as she said it. Daisy grinned. Even that hurt. She grunted her way through the conversation, her eyes closed tight and her head still under the duvet. As she became more conscious and the spinning slowed she realised that her muscles were also aching, her feet were immensely sore and her skin felt greasy: Obviously the alcohol was wearing off and the true pain of her erratic dancing was coming into fruition. She doubted that she was the only one. As her mum chatted away, Daisy tried to slowly sit up, sensibly facing away from the window, she was not ready for bright lights again just yet. She reached into her bag and retrieved her pack of paracetamol. Without water, she eventually managed to swallow them, although one felt as though it was lodged in her throat. After a minor coughing fit and apologies to her mum, Daisy sent the children her love and tentatively edged her way to the bathroom. She splashed warm water on her pallid face and cupped a mouthful to try to dislodge the tablet.

Eventually she felt the tablet travel, seemingly sideways, in the right direction. She needed it to stop messing around and get to work on relieving the headache, which was worsening with every movement. She had forgotten the aftermath of drunken nights out, but the recollection was returning with vengeance. Daisy had to admit that she was feeling more than a little sorry for herself as she gingerly showered and dressed. She was in no way able to look into a mirror long enough to apply make-up so retrieved her cardkey and bag and made her way, delicately down to breakfast. Well, coffee; she had used up all the provided sachets in her room. She hoped her stomach would not react badly to the smell of cooked breakfast, even the thought of it made her stomach somersault. She placed her hand reassuringly on her belly, as she leant against the handrail of the lift.

Wearing her sunglasses, her fringe resting on the top of them, and feeling slightly more worse for wear, Daisy carefully made her way through the hotel lobby, the aroma of coffee guiding the way. After successfully retrieving a double expresso shot from the complicated machine, Daisy attempted not to breath in the smell of fried breakfast, but even holding her breath seemed an effort. Her whole body felt fragile and her head was muggy. She made her way across the room towards the sofa area but then decided a table might be a better idea; she needed the added support to hold her upright.

"Daisy," Georgie called across the room, half standing and waving frantically.

Slowly she aimed in the direction of the sturdy table and friendly face. She sat down carefully, the full damage of the toning tights had left her buttocks tender.

"Oh," exclaimed Georgie with a smirk, "I see you had a good night then."

"Mmm. Well I didn't bolt halfway through that's for sure." Daisy slowly slid her glasses up to rest on her head.

"I'm so glad you stayed, I bet it was nice to catch up with all your old friends."

"It was." She stirred in five sachets of sugar and sipped her drink. The caffeine rush was harsh but necessary; her punishment for how much alcohol she had consumed.

Georgie chatted away as she ate her breakfast. Daisy listened as best she could, now the ringing in her ears was slowly subsiding, while trying to avoid eye contact with the fried eggs on Georgie's plate. Finally, Georgie announced that she was off to see her daughter and granddaughter later. She bit her lip after she said it and was wringing her hands.

"That's great," exclaimed Daisy, slightly louder and upbeat than either of them expected. Maybe her ears were still blocked.

"Yes. It is, isn't it?"

Daisy was unsure as to whether Georgie was asking her if it was great or telling her. Daisy just smiled and placed her hand over Georgie's. Daisy looked her in the eyes.

"It will be fantastic, it will." She reassured her. She hoped that she was right. Georgie had travelled a long way and put a huge amount of importance in this all going well.

"I tell you what, text me before you go and once you are on your way back here. I'm heading for home in a couple of hours so we can catch up on the phone later and you can tell me what a fantastic time you've had."

Georgie gave her a grateful smile and squeezed her hand back. Daisy felt as though she had made a friend for life. As much as Daisy was itching to get home to safe ground and her children, she felt as though she was leaving Georgie in a vulnerable situation in which she would have liked to stay to offer support. However, a phone call was the most she could offer at this point in time.

Georgie seemed to abruptly change her entire mood, as though covering over her emotions, in an all-too-expert kind of way. It was clear to Daisy that she had spent most of her life doing exactly this.

"So how did it go last night? I want details…" She asked expectantly.

It was Daisy's turn to close up.

"Erm, yea it was nice."

Georgie eyeballed her, "Hmm."

Daisy smirked back at her, "What?"

"I feel there is a story behind this hangover."

Daisy laughed guiltily. "I don't know what gave you that idea." The pot plant to her left suddenly needed her immediate attention. Georgie leant forward to try to catch her interest back. She fake-coughed and Daisy sat back in a teenage, sulky, 'I don't want to talk about it' fashion.

"I will start to guess and make assumptions if you don't tell me," she threatened.

"Seriously, there is not much to tell. Moreover, the bits that might be of interest I can't remember. I know there were cocktails and a gorgeous barman. There was definitely dancing…" Daisy looked shocked as the recollection hit her, "…and my childhood sweetheart was there and… oh God… he took me back to my room and…" her hand covered her mouth, her eyes almost popping out of her head.

"What?" Georgie probed.

"I don't know. I don't remember anything past him taking me in the lift to go to my room… then I woke up this morning."

"Was he still there?"

"No, I don't think so." Her mind was racing; she was mentally going through the moments after she woke up. *Had he been there? Could he have stayed for a while and left? Could he have been in the bathroom? No, she had been in there. Shit. Why couldn't she remember what had happened?*

"I'm sure you would have remembered if he had been there."

"Yea…" Daisy answered unconvinced, her brain still working overtime to find some snippet of information that would either confirm or disparage her fears.

After much confusion and racking of her brain Daisy and Georgie drained their coffees, exchanged contacts details and bided each other well wishes and hugs. Daisy left the reception area feeling quite dejected. She hit the button to call the lift and leant against the wall, feeling as though the effort to stand up unaided was more than she could manage at that moment in time. She slipped her glasses back onto the arch in her nose. Georgie had looked gutted at the idea of being left to fend for herself but Daisy needed to get home. She missed her children so much and chatting to them on the phone was no consolation. Equally, she needed to be home in her own world, safe and away from past memories which had leaked their way into her present. She didn't so much regret coming, as she had enjoyed herself, met Georgie and filled her alcohol quota for the year in one night.

Chapter Eight- Beehive

Daisy couldn't sleep, this was starting to become a bad habit. She was laying in her own bed, in the safety and comfort of her own home but still sleep did not seem a viable option. Her mind was racing with the events of the weekend. It felt as though she needed to solve the puzzle of the missing few hours of her life. The drunken few hours, in which time, many things could have happened, none of which she could recall.

When she had returned home earlier that day she had been greeted with hugs, handmade cards, sticky cakes and fresh tea; not necessarily in that order. This was the welcoming she had envisaged on the long journey home, yearned for was probably a better description. Daisy had felt lost, as though she no longer cared what other commuters thought of her or what level of confidence she was or wasn't showing. She had needed to get home. To be embraced by her family. To feel sure of her footings once more. Yet this plan had been foiled by her mum leaving and the children eventually falling asleep; she had only had to read the Gruffalo three times.

The silence of the house had given her mind the time to get back to searching for the absent information which had been lost in transition between action and memories. She pondered, *whether she would actually want to remember the events of the night before. Maybe her brain was protecting her from these horrific details. However if her and Tristan had hooked up she would at least want to know about it. Wouldn't she? Oh God, she was never going to drink again. Well… she was never going to attend a stupid reunion again or anything involving any ex of any kind. Or beautiful angelic barman.*

Daisy threw back the duvet with purpose and reached for her dressing gown. She switched on all the lights as she made her way through to the kitchen.

Leaning against the side while the kettle busied itself with the task of boiling water at this ungodly hour, her mind returned to its task. *Bottom line is did I have sex? Was it with Tristan? Was it good? No,* she reprimanded herself, *that is not at all the point. Technically if it had been that earth shattering the chances where high that she would have sobered up at some point during the proceedings, at least long enough to have orgasmed.* Something which she would welcome a reunion for! *Obviously,* she concluded as she poured the hot water the tea bag, *she had merely passed out and he had put her to bed. Shame. Crap.* That was not the kind of thoughts she wanted to be having about bloody-godforsaken-still-as-yummy-as-ever Tristan. *Shit.*

She cradled her cup in her hands and wandered back to her bedroom, popping her head round on each of the children as she went. She wished life was as simple for her now as it had been at their age. In fact, she wanted nothing more than to scoop them both up in her arms and lay with them close. Instead, she left them to enjoy a restful sleep and put 'Leap Year' on the DVD player in her room. Ten minutes after finishing her tea, Daisy drifted into a restless sleep, awaking intermittently to what seemed like the same point in the film.

Daisy awoke to the unfamiliar sound of silence. Momentarily she was panicked. She reached for her phone, 5.29am. She dropped it back onto the bed and buried her head into her pillow. It was too early, even for a Monday. But apparently her mind had decided she had had enough sleep for one night and refused to go back. Now she needed a wee. This was not a good start to her day, she hoped it was just a minor blip.

The children found Daisy asleep at the kitchen table, one hand still grasping her cold coffee. Her head planted firmly on Sally's Barbie table mat. For a moment they just observed her quizzically but soon grew uninterested in her, she did less than the iguana they had seen at the butterfly park. The children scuttled busily around her, preparing their cereal. It was only once the milk, which had not been properly deployed into Cory's bowl, seeped slowly across the table and reached Daisy's hand that she became aware of the children's presence. She lifted her head and focused her sleepy eyes.

"Morning guys."

"Morning mum, are you ok?" enquired Cory.

"Yes, Sweety, I was just tired because I woke up very early."

Daisy rose from her chair slowly and on autopilot fetched the cloth and bleach and cleaned the milk from the table.

"Sorry Mum," apologised Cory.

"No worries, honey." She smiled reassuringly at him, his Dad would not have reacted quite so calmly and the children were still weary of the reaction to bad behaviour. He was not the smacking type but he shouted, quite loudly and unnecessarily. Daisy, however, was a calm mother, most of the time, things like spillages or broken items were part and parcel of her day and not worth getting stressed about. This morning she did not have the energy to get worked up over it, she just dealt with it and made a coffee.

Seemingly hours later Daisy and the children were showered and dressed and snuggled up watching 'Nanny McPhee', in her opinion the best kids film ever. Many a time she had wished for the help of her or any Nanny for that point. Days like this were few and far between but the handy May bank holiday was worth more to her than just catching up with her maypole dancing. Today it was a well-deserved catch up day with her children. They had a feast of popcorn and giant smarties and she had kept the coffee flowing in order to stop herself falling back to sleep. The duvets had been dragged into the lounge and it was perfect.

They all jumped as Daisy's mobile violently vibrated on the arm of the sofa and they giggled at how silly they were. Sally passed it to her and she nipped out of the room to answer it, the film was at a vital part, the children had just learnt to use their manners.

"Hello."

"Hello, is that Daisy?"

"Erm, yes. Who is this?"

The man cleared his throat. "It's Tristan."

Daisy nearly dropped the phone, her mouth agape.

"How did you get my number?" she asked, glancing back towards the lounge door. Nanny McPhee struck the floor with her stick.

"You gave it to me the other night after I took you to your room."

"Did I?"

"Erm, yes. Sorry is this a bad time?"

"No… I mean… erm… I just hadn't realised… remembered… that I had given it to you." The more casual she tried to make her voice sound, the more she tripped over her own words. She stood in front of the kitchen mirror, watching the shock and awkwardness of this moment etch across her face. She nervously tucked her fringe behind her ear. She could hear the children starting to get restless. She bit her lip, this was not a welcome or comfortable situation. Why could he not have stayed and spoken to her the night of the reunion rather than disappearing all night, only to return for whatever it was they did or did not do together. She inhaled deeply, bracing herself to confront him. Put her mind at rest one way or the other.

"So…"

"Can we meet up?" he burst out over her imminent questioning. The words she had planned to say stuck in her throat as she reassessed the contents of his call and the obvious amount of courage he had seemed to have worked up in order to call her.

"Erm… I… hmm… I don't know… to be honest…" God she was useless at this stuff.

"Daisy. I just meant a coffee. Just a catch up, nothing odd or weird, I just wanted to talk to you properly." He cleared his throat, "I was disappointed that you had left London before I had a chance."

Her head was spinning, there was the distant sound of cushions thumping heads emanating from the living room. She knew she needed to answer him but what would she say? She met her eyes in the mirror. She looked tired, scared and sad, lonely maybe.

"Yes." *Shit, did she actually say that out loud?*

"Cool, thanks mum," a happy Sally skipped past her to get more popcorn.

"Excellent, I'm in Lynn Wednesday, catching up with my Dad. Are you free then?"

Daisy was trying to whisper to Cory to get him to put the popcorn back. He was having none of it. Tristan was rattling on about something to do with Wednesday. She was making all the right noises while practically wrestling Cory to the floor.

"Sure yes great, I'll text you tomorrow night to confirm."

"Ok."

"Good, bye. Look forward to seeing you."

He cheerily rang off. Daisy let go of Cory and allowed him to run off with the snack. She sat on the cold tiled floor, her palms to her forehead, elbows on her knees. The children were quiet again; only the sound of rustling popcorn and the film soundtrack echoing down the hallway broke the loud silence. Daisy was struggling to breathe. *Had she just agreed to go out with Tristan? All it had taken was him to catch her off guard and Cory to sneak past seeing her while she was not concentrating… sneaky, very sneaky… both of them!*

Just as she was peeling herself from the floor her phone beeped informing her she had a text message. She took a deep breath. *Surely he wasn't that keen.* But fortunately it was from Georgie. She relaxed her shoulders and wandered back towards the living room to join the children. 'Beehive' they were saying along to the film, 'beehive'. Daisy smirked and made a buzzing noise at them, making them chuckle.

The text read 'All went well. It was so great to see them. Now on my way back to Lincoln. Was great to meet you and hope to be able to meet again very soon. Georgie x'

Daisy replied. 'I'm so very pleased for you, glad it all went well. Yes, we will definitely have to catch up soon. Daisy x'

She smiled to herself as she snuggled back in with the children, stealing a smartie as she did so. They moved in closer and she felt as though life was perfect. *But what was going to happen about Tristan?* She pushed the thought to the back of her mind, where he deserved to be and laughed along to the 'cake fight' part of the film. Watching her children giggling she felt complete as though this moment would be held forever in her heart and soul, her own little moment file, to recall at will when things got bad. Nevertheless, for now in this moment she could stay, if only for a few minutes. She munched contently on her giant smarties.

Chapter Nine- Facing Your Fears

Wednesday came around all too soon, Daisy made her way slowly through the morning traffic in King's Lynn. She had to admit that she had not missed fighting her way through this every day but today was different. *Today was purely sociable and innocent. It was just coffee. In the light of day and with an old friend.* Well, ex-boyfriend but seeing as so many years had passed, Daisy preferred the term 'old friend' it made her feel as though it was less serious. This train of thought however was not helping her palms to stop sweating or her stomach to cease its somersaults. She wiped her hands down her jeans. She breathed deeply, trying to calm herself but the not-too-dissimilar feelings were taking over. She hated the fact that she got so nervous. It was stupid. She had only seen Tristan less than a week ago, so there were no major reasons to worry.

She turned up the car radio to drown out her panicking inner-monotone or 'chatterbox' as Susan Jeffers used to refer to it. Yet as loud as she sung she was still tempted to just text and cancel. But once Daisy said she was doing something the guilt of not doing it got to her and she followed it through no matter how uncomfortable she felt. As she parked up her legs were like jelly, she willed her body not to let her down now. Somehow she managed to get her ticket and fetched her bag from the footwell of the car. Another very deep breath and she marched off, looking as confident and purposeful as she could. Her trip to London had taught her that, if nothing else. Pretending to be confident was her new 'thing'.

Turning the corner, she saw him instantly, sat in the sun as though it had been designed solely to shine on him and all his grandeur. Her throat made an involuntary noise, not unlike a gagging sound. There was no denying he was a stunning specimen of a man but his narcissistic side shone through strong for her as she knew him better. He was fully aware of the attention he was getting and he revelled in it. She could turn around now and run, save herself the agony of having to place herself in his presence and subject herself to the all too familiar looks from other people which said 'really you are with her?' Daisy was not so sure she could handle this. *Could they not have found somewhere which would have been slightly less public, like a dark corner of the M&S foodhall?* She knew, however, that no matter where they went she would feel the same and no amount of lighting variables would save her from her own feelings for him.

"Daisy. I'm so pleased you made it." He stood to pull out a chair for her and after checking her preference made to go get her a drink.

In his absence, she changed her seating position many times in order to look less frumpy or tense. None of them seemed to work, as her stance was not going to change her perspective of herself. She was disappointed that she baited to his every whim, even after all these years. And even more so that she had wanted to see him at the reunion and for him to ring her and to meet him today. She finally settled in having her handbag placed on her lap to cover the majority of her bulging stomach and crossed her legs to make them look less chubby. Yet, as he returned, placing her cappuccino in front of her, he was looking only at her eyes. She froze. They froze. Caught in their own still-frame. *What was the rule? Don't make eye contact? Don't show fear? Or was that dogs?* She figured that the same rules applied to exes… old friends.

She thanked him as he sat back down and smacked the sugar sachets on the edge of the table, tore them open and tipped them carefully into her drink; her hands were giving away her emotions again, sweaty and shaky now. She quickly stirred it and sat back to observe the passers-by.

"I'm sorry about the other night by the way."

She turned to face him, but said nothing. How could she when she had no idea what he was referring to?

"I didn't mean to scoop you away like that, it was just that you seemed… like you need assistance," he finished.

She nodded and sipped her drink, hoping no froth would stick to her upper lip.

"Not that you are incapable… more that you had drunk quite a lot… obviously most people had but…" he looked uncomfortable, unsure almost of how to carry on. "I just thought it was for the best to get you safely to your room. I still care for you, you know, to ensure you are safe."

Daisy tried to speak but no words escaped her gaping mouth. She cleared her throat instead. He seemed to be concerned by her response but reached for his cup instead of speaking. After a few moments of stirring her drink and making patterns in the foam, Daisy addressed him, her head still down.

"What did happen that night Tristan? As you said, I had drunk a lot, but I woke up slightly confused, to say the least." She grimaced at her own bad behaviour as her eyes meet his, searching in them for the answers he might have.

He rubbed the back of his neck, "Erm, I just put you to bed." A grin spread across his face, "Did you think… that we… no, no not even close. Honestly, you were safe. You drunkenly scribbled your number down and pretty much passed out once we got to your room, I just laid you on the bed and covered you up."

Daisy's expression softened, pure relief washed over her and in place of it, her face flushed with embarrassment.

"Well, thank you." That was the best she could say in the circumstances. She continued drinking her coffee, as did he.

"You did look beautiful the other night though."

Daisy nearly spat her mouthful all over him. *What was he doing, testing her endurance of inappropriate phrases? If so, she was failing miserably.*

"That's very kind of you to say so. So did you, I mean handsome." *God this was the most awkward conversation ever.* She would quite willingly revisit the past and once again sit in on the confession of Joel's sexual orientation.

Daisy finished her drink. "So, it is nice to see you again so soon but may I ask what the purpose of this catch up is?"

He seemed momentarily stumped, but made a quick recovery.

"I just wanted to see you again and my visit was planned weeks ago, I thought I'd see if you were free. Sorry if I have made you feel uncomfortable, that was not my intention."

"It's ok, the nerves are wearing off." She giggled, trying to lighten the mood.

"Do you fancy a walk?"

"Yes, I do actually." She put her bag strap over her shoulder and stood, waiting for him to gather his belongings. He had obviously got into town early as he had a couple of shopping bags with him.

They walked through the town and out along the riverside. They discussed trivial things such as the boats, ducks, the modern art sculptures, but Daisy felt as though he had an ulterior motive to meeting up with her. She tried not to dwell on it and hoped that it was just her nerves that were causing her to think so negatively about his reasons. They stopped on a bench halfway along the dock and stared silently out across the river Ouse and the edges of West Lynn. Daisy checked her phone, nothing. Right now she could have done with a text from her Mum or an emergency phone call from the school, not that she wished her children harm so that she had an excuse to leave, but well.

Tristan broke the silence.

"I have thought about you over the years, wondered how you were getting on; if you were married, had children, that kind of thing."

"Really?"

"Yea, I missed having you in my life, you were such a big part of it for so long."

"Yea I guess I was." Daisy tried to play it cool. Pretend that she had not thought of him too. Until she knew his reasons she did not want to divulge too many of her inner thoughts or emotions. The ribbon on the box was not ready to be untied or even loosened as of yet. She had made that mistake before with him, proclaimed her love and had her heart broken. Instead, she simply nodded along again as he spoke of asking friends about her and looking in the paper for mentions of her, wedding or birth announcements, while he was visiting his parents. He confided that while in relationships with others he had wished that they were her. When imagining having children she was the mother he could imagine his children to have.

Daisy felt herself stop breathing and her heart was beating faster. She wanted nothing more than to agree, to say she had done the same but no, she couldn't not yet. He had betrayed her trust one too many times. If he pined for her it was nobody's fault but his own. He had been given the opportunity to have her forever. They had proclaimed as much in letters and postcards when away from each other and then while staring passionately into each other's eyes. It felt like a lifetime ago but then she guessed it was. They had talked for hours about their future together and their wedding and children's names. Her soul ached for those times, they had been so happy, so in love.

She straightened up; both physically and mentally. *Who did he think he was? Swanning back into her life just as she was trying to rebuild it for herself and her children after another man had let her down! How dare he sit here remorseful and pitiful, reminiscing about the time before he had shattered her soul into a thousand pieces, some of those pieces were never even found and had left an empty gaping pit of nothing inside her. Whenever things had felt as though they were slightly similar to those situations later in life those gaps became canyons which swallowed up her self-confidence and strengths and she inwardly fell into those pits of despair which he had created and left unknowingly. So while he pined she suffocated in her own fears.*

She suddenly got to her feet, defiance etched across her face.

"I have to go, I will see you later."

"What? I… erm… ok. It was great seeing you again." She ignored his pleading eyes.

"Likewise. Goodbye. Thanks for the coffee." She added as she strutted away with a purpose to her that oozed composure and strength.

She got to the car ten minutes later, beads of sweat on her forehead and closed the car door and crumbled. She sobbed. She thumped the steering wheel. She wanted to return to him and rip his bloody head off! *How could he sit there expecting sympathy for how wrong his life turned out when he had caused it! What was he expecting her to say? Ahhhhhh.*

Mid-inner-rant there was a tap on the window, causing her to jolt and nearly chock on her own tears. She turned the key and pressed for the window to lower.

"Are you ok Mam?" It took every last part of her willpower not to leap out of the car and beat ten bells out of the traffic warden.

"I'm fine, thank you." Was her actual reply, painted with a fake smile for convincing's sake.

He smiled back and edged away, obviously seeing the death stare she was aiming at him. Well not at him per say but to all mankind… what a joke… mankind… manevil!

Chapter Ten- Living With Regret

Daisy arrived home no less distraught. She slammed her bag down on the kitchen table, unsure as to just what she was carrying in it as it sounded far louder than expected. She flicked on the kettle and paced like a wildcat. She had not been this angry in a long time. Even how long it was taking to make a coffee was annoying her. She blew her fringe out of her eyes, *stupid fringe.* Her coffee tasted bitter, she felt bitter. Part of her wanted to race back to where her mind still held him, to the bench on which he was probably still sitting, feeling dazed and confused at her sudden exit. *Good.* She hoped he was still freaked out. Why should she be the only one to feel it? She wanted to shout at him, to scream at him, to tell him exactly the way she had been feeling all these years. The longing she had felt for him. The loss at losing him in the first place, and then again.

She growled, irritated and frustrated at her lack of confidence to face up to him right when she had had the opportunity. But would she have stopped. There were so many repressed emotions inside her screaming to get out, to make him see that pain. The ribbon on her box had been ripped off with the force of the lid flying off. The opening of Pandora's box was nothing in comparison to the wrath he would suffer if she ever set eyes on him again.

Daisy composed herself and fixed a smile to her face as she collected the children from school. There was no need to show them how upset she was and to be honest she felt a little bit as though saying it out loud would sound ridiculous. Thinking back he had said nice things, showed her he still cared. Somehow, that had made it worse. She considered it might be easier to cope with rejection if he had just not cared about her. It unsettled her to know that when she had daydreamed about him he had been thinking of her right back. *Had their thoughts connected with each other somewhere in the universe so as to bring their souls back together now?* She shook her head. *No, they had not. He was just an arse!*

"Why are you shaking your head mummy, don't you like my painting?" a sad face with a wobbly bottom lip asked her.

"Oh no, honey I was shaking my head at that car parked across the school gates again." She bent down and placed her hands on his shoulders, the throng of parents and children pushed against them as they stopped. "Your picture is beautiful, is that a smiling sun?"

His face brightened, "No mummy, it is a picture of you… a poortrain!" He explained with pride.

"A portrait! Of me, wow! Look how big and bright my smile is."

The throng pushed them towards the car. She had not felt like the walk today, she had no energy left. Cory's picture had cheered her up so much. The power of a child. She mirrored her portrait, a shiny smile beaming, and turned to ask Sally how her day had been. The children chatted away to her as they waited for the traffic to clear, as they made their way home, and as they sat at the kitchen table, chocolate around their mouths. This part of the day was Daisy's favourite. She loved hearing the chattering of her children, the gossip, the fun, the upsets, the details of their little lives. She kissed them both on the tops of their heads and squeezed them tight. Daisy dipped a chocolate digestive into her coffee and listened intently to them.

"How was your day Mummy?" enquired Sally

"It was ok, thank you, I went to King's Lynn for coffee." She swallowed hard.

"On your own?"

"No… with an old friend actually… who I met in London."

"Who?" asked Sally.

"Tristan."

They both looked at her simultaneously. Daisy gulped.

"Cool name." commented Cory

Daisy smiled wide. Her children were so fab. They were the reason she had no regrets in life. The reason she was not the one sat on the riverside feeling sorry for herself and how life had treated her unfairly. She had been blessed. She had two beautiful children. Obviously, her marital status was not as stable as she had hoped but she had gotten more out of the marriage than she had lost. She was not in the slightest bit regretful.

Daisy and the children had a relaxed afternoon. They played 'Monopoly Crazy Cash' and cooked fajitas for dinner. Sally helped her chop up the salad and Cory had fun squeezing the sour cream and salsa sauce into bowls. Daisy could not help her mind from wandering and was pleased with her current company. The bedtime routine was fast approaching and it held dread for her, the last thing she needed at this point was the eerie silence that filled the end of her day. It was at these moments, as she pottered around the house, tidying, washing-up, collecting the dirty washing, and scraping toothpaste off the mirror/taps/floor, that she did most of her thinking. Tonight she didn't want to think. She might get an early night or find that half-read book she had laying around somewhere.

In the meantime, she got the children's pyjamas ready and found them both a towel. While they took it in turns to swim in the tub, Daisy cleaned the toilet. As the children had grown older they had expressed their need for privacy, which Daisy fully respected, however her fear of leaving them in the bath alone was still taking time for her to adjust, so instead she did little jobs in the bathroom or very nearby. She covered her eyes if she had to be in view of them, at which point they giggled at her silliness, and the many near-collisions with doors or walls, most of which were not acted.

As she dried their hair in turn she put on her best Essex accent and enquired as to where they were heading on their holidays and how their children were. They loved it when she did this and were most disappointed when she forgot to give them the full hairdressing experience. Finally, while they cleaned their teeth and argued over the towel, Daisy collected their clean school uniforms and hung them on their door handles. She placed their bookfolders by the front door and gathered up their wet towels and discarded clothing.

Eventually they were tucked up in bed and she kissed and cuddled them and settled on the hallway floor to read them a bedtime story. This had become even more important to both her and them since Joel had left. To her it symbolised the end of her mother role for the day and to them it showed that no matter how tired or busy she was, she always had the time to read to them. Tonight it was 'Jack Sprat'; this had been her copy from her own childhood and was a cherished item by all of them. They all knew the words off by heart and the children would say parts aloud before she had even turned the page. She finished the book and doled out more kisses and cuddles.

"Night, love you, sweet dreams."

"Night, love you, Mummy."

"Love you, night, sweet dreams."

The ritual of putting the house back together began. Luckily most of it was done because Daisy tended to be an emotional-cleaner. This worked in her favour most of the time as she thrived on stress but when she was relaxed the house suffered. Obviously this was the point people decided to visit.

She was just sitting down to read her book, which had turned up on the DVD shelf of all places, when her phone bleeped. She vowed to ignore it, she had only just calmed down. But curiosity got the better of her and she opened the text.

'I hope you are ok. I enjoyed our catch up. See you soon I hope. T x'

She replied with a simple, 'Yes. Thanks. ☺'

Putting her phone down she couldn't concentrate on her book. She cursed under her breath and then picked her phone back up.

'Hiya, are you free for a chat?'

Her Mum replied instantly, 'YES' she was still very much excited by this amazing technology and although she could only type in capitals and very slowly, she loved it. They chatted for the allotted hour that BT allowed for free and Daisy felt much better afterwards. She had poured her heart out to her Mum who, having remembered the first-love stage of her teenage years was very understanding of Daisy's upset. Her advice was to either meet up again and tell him how she felt or let him know that she had no desire to see him again.

Daisy had smirked, these were of course the obvious choices and part of her had hoped that her Mum would tell her which one was best. But she knew that was neither her Mum's place or responsibility. Her upbringing had been one of make your own choices and deal with the consequences. Whichever way things turned out her parents where there to celebrate or commiserate accordingly. The older she got, it was not much different, other than the addition of proffered alcohol.

Daisy scooped up her belongings, locked the doors and turned off the lights. She needed to be safe in her bed, hide under the duvet and hope that tomorrow would be better. She kissed the children gently as she checked on them and repositioned their duvets. Right this moment she wanted nothing more than to curl up on the hallway floor, between their rooms and sleep; safe in the knowledge that they were close. It was nothing more than conditioning that lead her to sleep in her bed. She needed a hug so bad right now that she thought she might just burst into tears again.

It was these lonely moments when she missed Joel. However, she remembered that she had rarely shown how upset she was, so the hugs had been few and far between after the children were born and life got busy; right when she had needed his reassurance most. But tonight the man she craved comfort from was Tristan. She knew it made no sense. She knew that he was the reason she was feeling so down. But that was the point. She had missed him all these years, gone off to sleep wishing his arms were holding her tight. Her tears soaked into her pillow as she drifted off to sleep. *Why had he come back?*

Chapter Eleven- Fate Steps In

Arriving home from the school run Friday morning Daisy burst into tears again. She had held herself together yesterday while the kids were home because she had to. She had woken up with puffy eyes and feeling emotionally wrought. But as every mother does she had performed her duties, found her sunglasses and added extra concealer under her eyes, on top of the eye reviver. To finish off her morning routine she had reapplied her shiny smile. Yet the excess energy those tasks had taken caught up with her and knocked her off her feet. She sat huddled up behind the front door for what seemed like an age, just sobbing her heart out. The sleeves of her jumper were sodden and her head hurt from the exertion. It was only the post coming through the letter box, nearly impaling her head that broke her from her despair.

She stayed where she was and flicked through them. Right at the bottom of the junk mail and bank statements was a beautiful postcard of a cathedral, according to the back it was Lincoln Cathedral by night. Daisy genuinely smiled and read the card.

'Hi Daisy and children, I'm a traditionalist and love snail mail. Wanted you to see the gem of a city I was telling you about. I hope you have a chance to come visit soon, you are always welcome. Love & best wishes, Georgie xxx'

Daisy was a believer in fate and signs. She hauled herself off the floor and made her way through to the kitchen.

She texted, 'Thank you so much for the card, it is beautiful. Are you busy this weekend?'

This weekend was Joel's weekend with the children, they were picked up at 6pm on Fridays and dropped off Sunday at the same time. Daisy did not feel she could cope with being in the house alone this time, she felt the need to get away, going to see Georgie seemed like just the escape she needed.

After having successfully packed the children off to their Dad's for the weekend, Daisy braced herself ready to endeavour upon her journey up country to Lincoln. She was nervous, to say the least, but overriding those feelings was pure determinism. Her logical mind told her she was being reckless; picking up and leaving when she had so many jobs to do at home, her children might need her and she would be over an hour away, she didn't really know Georgie, she was technically a stranger. But Daisy knew in her heart that she could trust Georgie, she was the rare kind of person that you instantly connected with and instinctually trusted, and in her experience the majority of these specimens were female.

So, she had packed a weekend's worth of clothes, plus a bit extra, just in case. Her make-up bag & toiletries were repacked into her vanity case and a spare pair of shoes in case they ventured out for the evening. She had made a concerted effort to turn her nerves into excitement. After years of being married this going away for the weekend, alone, was a new phenomenon, but one that she was resolute to get used to and to do more often. She had many friends scattered about the country whom she could pop and visit. She decided to make a pact with herself to have one weekend away a month and then one at home, while the children spent time with their Dad. It was, after all, 'her time'; again something she was trying very hard to adjust to.

Heading into Lincolnshire on the A17 Daisy sung along to the radio. She was unaccustomed to long drives, as much as weekends away. Joel had always done the majority of the drives, especially the long drives. She had, however, doubled checked her AA membership and her fluids and tyre pressures on her car before setting off. She had even treated herself to a new air freshener, shaped like a lizard. She named it Iggy. The new chapter of her life was beginning and so far she was loving the way it was going. She was making her own decisions. The children were doing well in themselves and the time she spent with them was so much calmer and happier.

This was not to say that life with Joel had been overly stressful or full of angst but towards the end of their marriage it was, strained, more of an effort to be relaxed and happy around each other. She had dreamt of contentment, more time for each other, maybe weekends away like this would have helped. She knew her Mum would have been more than happy to have babysat for them. But inevitably the truth of their discontent had been revealed and if nothing else, Daisy could rest safe in the knowledge that no matter what she had done or who she had become, he was gay. She was not the problem in their marriage, his sexual orientation was the elephant in the room, having squeezed its way out of the closet. So between them they had broached the elephant and dealt with it the only way you could with an issue this big; one bite at a time.

In all fairness, they were good friends, they always had been and she hoped they always could be. It was not a clash of personalities or money strains, it was purely and simply a difference in their sexual needs. Daisy had to respect him for dealing with the situation, even if it had taken him a while, but it showed that they had been strong in the fact that he felt he could be honest with her. They had talked it through, worked out the visitation with the children, the separation of the finances and the living arrangements. They had both opted for a fresh start. He got himself a flat in town and she had bought a house just two roads away, nearer the school and on a bus route. It was not to say that none of it had been painful, upsetting or that they hadn't screamed and balled at each other; of course they had.

But the be all and end all was that they both wanted what they had always wanted; to be happy and in that their children would be happy.

The traffic was surprisingly light for a Friday evening and Daisy drove along excited to meet up and explore the city with her newfound friend. This was what it was all about, stepping out of her comfort zone, seeing and experiencing different things. Taking chances and allowing fate to guide her rather than trying to control fate and telling it what she wanted. She approached the final roundabout and took the 4th exit to Lincoln. The views were stunning as she wove her way along the road and up and down the hills. As she came down one of the hills she had to quickly swerve to avoid a peacock that had wandered out of a driveway and into the road. A few sharp bends and an airbase later and she was entering Bracebridge Heath and the descent into Lincoln City.

The sun was still shining and evening was fast approaching. The lighting surrounding the Cathedral was breathtakingly beautiful and it was all she could do to keep her eyes on the road. The Cathedral stood proud, as it had done for centuries, overseeing the comings and goings of the world around it. Georgie had not been kidding when she said it was a beautiful city. Now she was in Lincoln she had to navigate her way through it to Georgie's house. Easier said than done. After driving on her brakes down into the city, she was now moving along at a snail's pace down the main road into Lincoln. This did however give her the opportunity to see what was around. She was surprised at how many sculptures there were; instead of railings there were metal leaves upon stalks, and many of the buildings had figures carved into their architecture.

She was meeting Georgie in the Toys-R-Us car park, which according to her directions was just at the top of the road, turn left at Tesco Express, then second left, can't miss it! Apparently. After two extremely complicated manoeuvres, and slightly nifty, even if she did say so herself, she found the car park. With sheer relief she saw Georgie, leant against her car, sipping a Costa coffee and beaming from ear to ear. Daisy dragged her wobbly limbs and numb bottom from the car and headed in her direction. Georgie met her halfway and they hugged.

"That was insane!" declared Daisy dramatically wiping her brow, "I remember now why I don't ever drive anywhere outside a ten mile radius of my house. I'm such a bumpkin these days."

Georgie laughed, "You get used to it. Let's get you a coffee."

They locked up the cars and strolled into the City centre, it was quite a trek. Arriving at Costa Daisy placed herself in the comfiest seats available, while Georgie ordered them a Mochachocalatte and a big slice of chocolate cake. Daisy knew why she had made friends with this wonderful woman and felt that heading up here for the weekend was in fact the best decision she could have made. What were her other options? To have sat and wallowed in her own self-pity and then to have text Tristan in a moment of weakness? That would have been her biggest mistake. What she actually needed was this; a fab friend, great coffee and cake and a friendly nonbiased viewpoint on her ridiculous situation. Which when she mulled it over now, seemed stupid and almost self-inflicted.

A smiling Georgie weaved her way through the tables and placed the yummies on the table.

"It is so great to see you," declared Georgie, seating herself opposite Daisy.

"You too, thank you so much for letting me come up at such short notice."

Georgie waved her comment away, "Not at all, this is great!"

"It is," confirmed Daisy. She felt herself welling up. She had needed to get away far more than she realised. They smiled at each other. Both knowing they needed one another's company even more than they were willing to express. Daisy sometimes hated being a part of the supposed power-woman generation. The exhausted-took-on-too-much-generation more like!

"So…" inquired Georgie.

Daisy knew this moment would come, she smiled wearily, "Hmm, Tristan. You know the ex from the reunion… we met up."

Georgie gave her an intrigued/concerned smile. "I see."

"Well, afterwards I was furious! All the emotions of the past came rushing back and smacked me full on in the face! I had spent years longing to see him again, I think even so much as to say, it was highly probable I was still in love with him, or at least the idea of him. But the reality of the situation was not the same as I had expected. Far from it, in fact. The script was the same…" she glanced over her shoulder as a giggling young couple passed behind her. Tears pricked her eyes. "I had yearned for him to say the things he did. Yet when he actually said them, I was so angry at him, at myself for allowing him even the chance to say them. Maybe it was a case of wanting it to stay as a 'maybe'." She made quote marks with her fingers as she said it. "I think he may have broken my heart all over again."

It was only as Georgie passed her a napkin that she realised that tears were running down her cheeks as she voiced her distresses. This had not been the plan. She had wanted to get away for the weekend, to step out of her life for a snippet of time, not sit here like a blubbering wreck in public. However, she rationalised, maybe this was what she needed. A friendly space in a strange place without the criticisms of people who knew her or the chance of bumping into someone she knew.

Georgie sat quietly, contently sipping her coffee and picking off bits of her cake, allowing Daisy to pour her heart and soul out.

After many concerned looks, which she didn't even acknowledge, Daisy calmed down. She had told Georgie the gist of the story of her and Tristan's past and of her present day feelings towards being back in contact with him. The bottom line was that he had loved her but not wanted to be a part of her life again until he chose to and after everything they had gone through all those years ago Daisy was scared that her already fragile heart could not take another beating from either him or Joel. She had wanted, no needed, to get strong again. To prove to herself and her children that she was not the crumbling mess that either man had left in their wake. Yet here she was in the throes of sobbing in the middle of Lincoln.

Her drink was now cold but she drunk it anyway, she figured that if she was to squirt cream on top and pop in a straw it was technically marketable as a Frappè.

"Let's walk," piped up Georgie.

Deja vu.

"We'll just head back to the cars and you can follow me back to mine, we could order out and chill for the evening. Then I thought we could make Steep Hill our mission for tomorrow," Georgie gestured it the direction of the cars and then Steep Hill which was behind them, almost taking out the eye of a passer-by. They both apologised and giggled.

Linking arms, they made their way through the city centre. Daisy stared at all the buildings, a bizarre mixture of historic and modern architecture. Somehow it worked, it suited the city, almost made it as it was. The daytime consumers had made way for the night-owls; young and old people out for the night, to drown their sorrows or dance away their cares. Daisy almost wished she had the energy or enthusiasm to join them, but tonight a relaxing evening at Georgie's with good company and junk food seemed like the perfect antidote to her worries.

Chapter Twelve- Making New Friends

Daisy's eyes flew open. It was quarter past two in the morning. Her heart was racing, the back of her neck was damp with sweat and her fringe was glued to her forehead. She gasped for breath in her disorientated state. She had awoken after a vivid dream of Tristan, heartbroken that it had only been a dream. In the dream they had been young again. They were sat on the bench by the river and they were laughing and joking. His arm was laid across her shoulders and she was snuggled into his chest. She was seeing it from an observer's point of view, looking longingly at the happy couple who were so obviously in love. The sense of security and togetherness overwhelmed her, awake now she could still felt it. As tears overwhelmed her once more, the realisation struck her as to why she had been so angry at his reappearance in her life. It was only now, laying in Georgie's spare room that Daisy realised she was angry because, every day of her life since Tristan had no longer been a part of it, she had missed him. His arms no longer wrapped around her when she stirred in the night, or his kisses on her shoulders as she drove. His reassuring hand on the base of her back or in the glint of his smile that informed her that she was safe. The emotion of this stuck in her throat and she felt dizzy.

No matter where or who she was or had been so far, he was there like this shadow from her past haunting her, taunting her with what she didn't have now but had once known.

She hugged her pillow tight and the realisation hit her that at times of anxiety in her life she had done exactly this; the mind had taken her back to the one person whom she had truly loved. It was only now that she considered whether she too had married Joel, as he had her, for comfort, to try to escape what she truly felt. To make up for the lost love which her heart and soul still yearned for. As much as Joel had married her knowing that he much preferred male company, she had committed to him knowing that her heart belonged to someone else. Freud may have been right in his wish fulfilment, she wished for Tristan, and her dreams were the only place they could truly be together.

Daisy leaned over and switched on the lamp. As the light illuminated the room she relaxed. It was odd having these dreams, and stranger still waking up in a strange place, but Georgie's house was a home in every sense of the word. It was nothing spectacular, just a simple three bedroom terrace just off Monk's Road. She had a flair for colour and objects which made you feel comforted. Even in the room Daisy was occupying there were trinkets on the windowsill and arty canvasses hung on the wall. The bookshelf was loaded with many differing genres of books and the bookends were colourful and fun.

Georgie's home was a montage of years of collecting bits and bobs, some of which her children had probably bought her for special occasions or made at school. In the hallway, as Daisy had climbed the stairs to bed, she had felt as though she was taking a journey through Georgie's life. Photos hung higgledy-piggledy on the wall, baby photos and young Georgie hugging what she assumed where her parents. Then a slightly older Georgie on her wedding day, then cradling a baby. School photos of smart, smiley children. Daisy felt as though just visiting her house meant that she knew Georgie better, her house was a true reflection of her personality, the events which had filled her life with happiness and sadness.

In the silence of the night Daisy crept back down the stairs to the bathroom. Being an old house the stairs where not accommodating to her desire to not disturb Georgie. Daisy bit her lip with every step, trying her hardest not to put too much weight on each step. She smirked at the thought of Georgie's daughter, Casey, as a teenager trying to sneak out to meet up with boys or for a midnight snack. This was the perfect staircase for a mother of teenagers. She made a mental note to buy a house with a creaky staircase before her children reached high school age; the noisier the better.

Finally, she made it through the kitchen and into the bathroom. She looked pale and puffy from all the crying and the lack of sleep. She splashed water on her face to try to revive herself. Her heart still felt heavy from her dream and she had an overwhelming urge to text Tristan to see if he too was awake in the early hours; possibly after experiencing a similar dream about her. But she was not going to start back on that train of thought. After a night of pouring her heart out to Georgie and then having a bloody good laugh together, she would not allow her melancholy side to take over again.

She decided that a hot drink would help soothe her and she might peruse the bookshelf in the bedroom when she went back to bed. Even if it took her a while to go back to sleep she would not feel quite so on edge if she had a good book to read. She filled the kettle and found a cup. The kettle sounded so loud in the quiet and she willed it to hurry up so she could get back to her warm bed. Even now, Daisy was not keen on the dark or being up alone in the night. As a child she had been chastised for her silliness and believed she would soon grow out of it. Yet, here she stood, still afraid. She tried to rationalise it to being in a strange place but she knew that she was equally as bad at home, if not worse.

She settled back in bed minutes later and sipped her tea. Her mind was starting to clear, the images from her dream dissipating. The dream had been so vivid, the feelings so strong. She tried to steer her mind away from it. Instead, she nestled the copy of 'Woman to Woman' by Cathy Kelly into her lap and started to read. The easy flowing prose pushed the thoughts of Tristan away and as she finshed her tea and then slid further down under the duvet, the book resting next to her on her pillow, her eyelids started to close. Sleep soon took over.

After a late breakfast, Georgie and Daisy made their way into the city. Daisy had confided in Georgie about her dream, she was a great listener. Daisy found that it helped to have talked it through, although she was still experiencing flashbacks. She always found it unsettling on days like this, when a dream stayed and haunted her, almost as though her mind was still trying to comprehend the events of the past few weeks. She was aware that the reunion would have stirred up all kinds of feelings from her past but Tristan's appearance had shaken her ontological security beyond compare.

Their trip into town was helping to ease her raw emotions; the two of them laughed and revelled in each other's company and not for the first time Daisy knew that her decision to visit Georgie was the right one. They skipped in and out of varying shops, holding up clothes the other one might like or hate, which they then ohed or ahed over accordingly. They chose jewellery, makeup and enjoyed rooting through bargain bins. Daisy was thoroughly enjoying herself.

Rounding the corner Georgie whooped with excitement, "Daisy, Daisy let's go in here, they have 25% off!" and off they jogged into Ann Summers. They giggled like school girls as again they held up outfits; maids, cheerleader, and many other differing quirky ensembles. Daisy started to feel a tad low again, looking at all these beautiful outfits wondering about the kind of men who liked them and more to the point the kind of women who wore them. Daisy inwardly cringed at the idea of ever trying to feel sexy in one of these, her rolls of fat would peep through the holes and as for ripping it off in the moment of passion, this PVC one which she was looking at, they would need some numerous tools to scrape it from her body! In her peripheral vision she saw Georgie disappear round behind a wall, then heard giggling, which broke her out of her inquisitive contemplation of sexual role playing and the logistics of such.

She meandered in the direction of Georgie, but gasped as she saw her, there she was, this middle-aged lady, shopping bag on one arm and handbag on the other, chuckling to herself. *What was that she was holding?*

"I love my new friend," she trilled in an American accent as she hugged the item, "he is so big," there was stroking, "I will love him and hug him and I will call him Tom." She thrust the biggest dildo Daisy had ever seen in her direction and laughed manically. Daisy roared with laughter also, once the shock passed. As she looked around her there were the weirdest, strangest shaped things she could ever have imagined. Her and Joel had never really ventured into the realm of 'play', apart from the fluffy handcuff presents on Valentine's day. She was genuinely intrigued, if not a little bit scared by what she saw. Georgie was like a child in a sweet shop and was thoroughly enjoying picking them all up in turn and switching the vibrators on. The shop assistant poked her head round and offered assistance but Daisy could tell by her eyes that she was taught to say that rather than considering the fact they might actually 'be needing' her advice or guidance. Daisy felt like a complete prude in here, way out of her depth.

Maybe this was what she needed, some hot steamy erotic sex with a willing participant. Not the assistant, obviously, but a willing man. Her mind wandered back towards Tristan and she considered whether he was into this kind of thing. For some unexplainable reason the thought of him experimenting with sex toys with other women upset her. To be fair, the thought of him with other women in general upset her, let alone the idea that he might 'be with her' as she hung from a swing, leather clad, and in thigh high boots. Ridiculously Daisy wanted to flee from the shop and these thoughts, she needed air.

"I'm just going to go get some fresh air."

"Ok," replied Georgie without looking round, she was crouched down investigating butt plugs and nipple clamps. Daisy gave a little grin, Georgie was so fun.

She willed herself to snap out of it and stop moping. *So what if Tristan was into kinky sex, who cares?* Daisy perched on the bench just along a bit. She was staring at all the ornate building and the archway and wondering about the history of Lincoln. She guessed it must have been extremely important to have had such a huge cathedral and a castle. Maybe she would Google it when she got home, it was at these times that she wished she had a nifty phone where she could check her Facebook and Google random facts. However she struggled with the one she had, setting the alarm or finding the calculator was difficult enough. Just as she was contemplating upgrading her phone, Georgie came running over proudly holding out an Ann Summers bag and announced to the entire street, "I bought Tom!" She had the biggest grin on her face and all Daisy could do was hug her and laugh along, if there was one line in the world that could snap someone out of there melancholy mood that was the one.

"Fantastic! Let's celebrate your new friendship with a couple of coffees."

"You know what? Neither of us are driving so why don't we go to Varsity for cocktails? I've heard they are delicious."

"Sounds like a plan." *What the hell, live a little, let your hair down, you deserve it!*

Chapter Thirteen- Liquid Lunch

"Wow! These are delicious!"

"Aren't they!" Georgie's eyes glinted over the top of her fishbowl glass as she sucked up the fabulous concoction.

This was the magic ingredient to her completely relaxing and forgetting all the crap. Life was really good, Daisy decided halfway down her drink. The children were amazing, healthy and happy. Her mum was also doing ok. She liked her new house, as did the children. She had caught up with a few old friends she might keep in contact with and she had found a wonderful new friend in Georgie, oh and Tom! She knew that soon enough she would come up with a job or at least an idea of the kind of job she wanted. Joel seemed settled in his routine with the children. It was good, very good, it was fab. Her drink was now empty and her smile was bigger than a Cheshire cat. Georgie's matched hers. They were happy.

The bag containing Tom had been laid on the table and as the waitress brought their drinks over and a bowls of chips, Georgie informed her that she must be careful of Tom, the waitress smiled and was careful. Daisy guessed she had heard many ramblings of drunkenness but if only she knew that Tom was not just the old woman's imaginary friend. Daisy could not stop laughing as the girl walked away and Georgie patted the bag to ensure his wellbeing.

The second drink did not go as quickly as the first, Daisy was not accustomed to mixing her drinks and her recent alcoholic behaviour was racking up some bad memories. She was going to pace herself, especially as it was only half past one in the afternoon. But to hell with it, she had a childfree weekend, no one knew her here and she could do as she pleased. She may even go and purchase the PVC outfit or her own Tom. She was feeling reckless and life was passing her by too quickly and all she ever seemed to do was 'be careful'. She lived in the 'what if' state, constantly worrying about the consequences but never really doing anything on the spur of the moment. She knew it was part of being a parent, to be responsible and think about the future. To make sure there was money in the bank for bills, food in the cupboard and the children were happy. *However, what about experiencing the fun stuff?*

"Excuse me," she slurred at the waitress. "Do you know where there is a good place to go out dancing?"

Georgie nearly spat out her drink with excitement, "Yes, good idea Daisy, let's get dressed up and go dancing!" Georgie was practically jumping up and down in her seat. Daisy felt she had made the right decision, dancing it was tonight then.

The young girl looked at them both and suggested, "Christopher's is good for ladies such as yourselves, cheap drinks and great music. Do you know where that is?"

"No, but it sounds perfect." Georgie piped up.

The waitress wrote down the directions on her notepad and advised them to go before ten, as it was free entry. They thanked her and tucked into their chips.

"I feel another shopping spree coming on," announced Daisy.

"Ooh, me too, we might find pretty dancing shoes like the ones in London but hopefully with a more reasonable price tag."

The two of them looked off into the far distance, the thought of beautiful shoes and a night of dancing ahead of them.

"Thank you so much for this," Daisy suddenly said, "You are so kind to let me stay, I'm so glad we met each other."

Georgie brushed the comment away with an overly enthusiastic gesture, "Me too." She reached for Daisy's hand and squeezed it, "We were meant to meet. Who would I go dancing with if not?"

Daisy had hit the emotion wall of her drinking, she still had half of it to go, so she hoped she would soon get to the jolly part. It had been a good idea to eat something, Lord knows how quickly the alcohol would have flooded her system if not. She was most certainly a cheap date.

Swinging Tom in the bag Georgie bounced along, the two of them linked arms as they made their way back up the High street. They considered their budgets and decided that Primark would be a good place to start their spree, cheap and cheerful. Neither of them wanted to blow their money on an outfit and shoes and struggle the rest of the month, as fun as this was, sensibility and practicality still won out. Just the petrol alone had put a dent in Daisy's budget, which was tight at the best of times. The London trip, even though she had saved up for it over a few months, had meant that there was no spare money that week and her Mum had kindly given her spending money, some of which had gone on last week's food bill. As much as she was determined to have a good time, she did not want to regret it later. From the way Georgie spoke, she was also on a limited budget so this shop would do nicely.

Some of the clothes were plain ugly and some too young for them but there were some really nice bits. They filled their baskets with options to try on and then aimed for the shoe department. Although the shoes were nowhere near on the scale of the London shop, there were some beautiful ones which would fit the occasion. In all honesty, Daisy did not want to spend the night worrying about dancing too much in case she sweated on her expensive dress or fretting over her shoes getting drinks spilt on them; she wanted to enjoy herself. So ten pounds on a pair of shoes and another tenner on an outfit was spot on. If they got wrecked she would not be best pleased but she would not cry for months wishing she had spent the money on food for the children, or in the case of the London shoes, a brand new sofa.

Georgie found some stunning white stiletto shoes with a neat buckle across the top. Most of the clothing she had chosen were light coloured so they were perfect. Daisy spotted some fabulous purple faux suede calf length boots, which matched a flowy dress she had fallen in love with. Excitedly the ladies made their way to the dressing room and tried on all their outfits and advised and laughed and cringed at each other's choices. After much fun, they both made a decision and headed to the checkout. The queue was quite long and Daisy and Georgie both spent a little bit more money on the trinkets they purposefully placed by the till points.

"Mam, Mam," called one of the shopping assistants running in their direction. "You left this in the changing room." She held out the Ann Summer's bag, blushing from ear to ear. Everyone turned to look at them.

Georgie calmly thanked her for returning Tom, Daisy was laughing so hard that she would definitely need to find a toilet when they got out of here. Daisy made a concerted decision, she would only shop after having consumed cocktails, they made the whole experience much more enjoyable. She wiped the tears from her eyes as they called her to the next available till. Behind her she could hear Georgie chatting away to the couple behind, explaining how relieved she was that Tom had not got left behind. The tears would not stop as she paid for her purchases. She nearly choked when she heard Georgie ask the older lady whether she had ever used a dildo, Daisy didn't dare turn around as she heard a rustling of a bag. *Please tell me she is not showing the lady Tom.*

Once they were outside and on their way to the nearest toilets Georgie was telling Daisy about how the lady in Primark was telling her about how a friend of hers who had once had a most upsetting experience with a man. "Apparently this friend of hers was in her seventies and having been recently bereaved and sort comfort in a gentleman friend of hers. Well, it only turned out that this man was extremely kinky. She said that, one evening her friend had been invited to his house for dinner. They got on very well and she enjoyed his company. But after they had loaded the dishwasher and he had made a pot of coffee he told her he wanted to show her something. The man popped off and returned with a suitcase. Obviously the friend was most intrigued and assumed it was old photos or his stamp collection. Do you know what it turned out to be?" Georgie's eyes were wide, she was also still a bit tipsy so was swaying slightly as she looked Daisy in the eyes.

"No," giggled Daisy, "What was it?"

"It was full of toys! Sex toys!" A few passers-by turned to look at them, Daisy could not meet their gaze.

"No?"

"Yep, this lady who I was just talking to received the phone call the very next day telling her all about it. He was a big fan of Viagra and pleasing a woman in many differing ways."

"What did the lady do?"

"Well, she finished her coffee, thanked him for dinner and left."

Daisy was off laughing again. "What did he do?"

"I don't know, but she sent him a text after talking to this lady, explaining that he was great company but she did not feel it would be respectful to her late husband to engage in sexual games at this time."

Daisy was roaring with laughter and she informed Georgie that she really, really needed to get to a toilet, like now.

Chapter Fourteen- Glad Rags

Unaccustomed to drinking in the afternoon the two of them fell asleep after their walk back. It was six thirty by the time Daisy stirred, her head feeling muggy and dozy. But her eyes fell on the brown paper bags by the bed and she smiled. She was really excited to be going on a 'proper' night out. She felt young again, full of vibrancy and expectation. *Was this the feeling she had been searching for? Yes, it was, this was how she wanted to feel again, as though life was full of possibilities and fun. That although she had no idea what the future held for her, sometimes it is exciting to just not know and look forward to the surprises that it holds.*

She could hear movement downstairs, she stretched. As she stood up, her calves burned, she hadn't realised how much walking they had done and her legs were not used to hill walking, in fact, she rarely did any other exercise than the school run these days, which did not involve any form of running whatsoever. She gingerly made her way down the stairs, holding on to the rail, she made a mental note not to put on her new boots until she was safely down the stairs later. She winced with every step until she finally reached the bottom.

"Oh my God my legs are aching after all the walking today."

"Really, how far did you go?" replied a male voice from behind the living room door.

Daisy took a sharp intake of breath and flushed bright red as the man met her in the doorway.

"What? Who? How?" mumbled Daisy, looking around frantically for Georgie.

"So my shoes are amazing, you wait until you see them," chimed Georgie from behind her. She was carrying two cups of tea and looked up to see Daisy's shocked face, "Oh, you are awake. I was just telling Stephan about our shopping trip."

Stephan? How was he here? Daisy was feeling completely disorientated, as though she had woken up in the wrong house. Stephan was now seated in the armchair, crossed legged and smiling at her. Daisy moved into the room to let Georgie through and sat heavily onto the sofa.

Seeing Daisy's confused state she introduced them properly. "Daisy this is Stephan, my nephew. Stephan this is my friend Daisy who I was telling you about, the one I met in London."

"Good to see you again."

"Er, yea, erm nice to see you again too." She knew she was blushing, her face felt as though it might melt under the heat.

"Oh do you two know each other?"

"Kind of," answered Stephan, Daisy seemed to have lost her voice.

"Oh how fabulous. How's that then?" she looked from one to the other.

"I also met her in London." He made eye contact with Daisy, a glint in them, which increased her temperature further. "You know I said that I was roped into doing the bartending that weekend you were down in London and you said it was a shame you didn't know because we could have travelled together? Well, your friend Daisy here was at the party I tended. I never forget a pretty face."

Holy shit! The room was spinning and Daisy felt that she may combust at any moment. *How the hell was he her nephew? Here in this house. Oh God.* The events of that night swam rapidly around her mind, the way he had kept an eye on her and brought her drinks over and how he had checked on her welfare when Tristan had taken her to the lift. She had never expected to see the angel barman again and had not considered that he might have a name. He seemed even more stunning sat here, the evening sun on his face from the window. *Maybe this is another dream?* She considered. At any time she might wake up.

"I'll get you a drink Daisy. Tea or coffee?" offered Georgie.

"It's ok, I'll make it. You two catch up." She scrambled to her feet, the pain shooting through her tired muscles. She stood in the kitchen, trying to get the thoughts straight in her head. *So, the angel barman was Georgie's nephew. He was here in her house and he remembered her, because he never forgot a pretty face.* Her knees went weak. She put the coffee and sugar in the mug and poured in the milk. *Here she was, miles from home, even further from London, only just relaxing and getting her thoughts straight about Tristan and this fantasy guy from the reunion turns up and calls her 'pretty'. He was probably just being polite because she was a friend of her aunt and he had to be at least ten years younger than her. No twentysomething was going to think she was pretty, let alone fancy her. She was obviously just still slightly tipsy and disorientated from her nap. But he had said she had a pretty face!*

Daisy added an extra spoonful of coffee to her mug, she needed to sober up and wake up quickly. She splashed cold water on her face and pulled herself together, as her mother would say. *She was a thirty-odd year old woman and in no way was she going to be intimidated by this fine specimen of a man. She would walk in there, act cool calm and collected and make idle chit-chat with him.* She composed herself and walked casually back into the room.

"I was just telling Aunt Georgie what an amazing dancer you are." *Composure lost.*

She smiled and nodded and sipped her drink, pretending that she had not just burnt her lip.

"Daisy and her friend did the dance to that old Mel and Kim song, it was very entertaining." He relayed to Georgie.

"How wonderful, we should request that tonight and you can teach me, I can't remember the last time I went out dancing."

If Daisy had been closer to him she probably would have kicked him. He seemed to be mocking her and she did not appreciate it. *She was fully aware of the fool she had made of herself that night, but he was partly to blame as he had supplied her with copious amounts of alcohol. Ok, he had not poured them down her throat but still, it was definitely his fault, and she held him responsible for Tristan. How that was his fault she was unsure at this precise moment, but she probably would not have allowed him or needed him to take her back to her room, thus giving him the impression that he could text her. Or in fact she would not have given him her number had she have stayed sober. However, if she had stayed sober she would not have made it through the night. Maybe he was not to blame.*

"Well I best go and get ready," announced Daisy once she had finished her drink.

Had her legs not been so painful she might have got up the stairs quicker, but as it was, it seemed to take forever. She wanted to hide in her room, she was not even thinking of the night ahead, all she could think about was Stephan, sat downstairs in all his grandeur. *Maybe he was into the kinky stuff? That would be a fantastic way to blow away some cobwebs. Stop it! Behave!* She told herself, *he is no more than a boy, hardly out of puberty. Well not quite that young but still.* She suddenly giggled to herself at what he would think of his aunt buying Tom.

Considering the inexpensive ensemble, Daisy was quite pleased with the effect. The dress hugged her and concealed her in all the right places and the length was flattering to her legs. She had applied her makeup and straightened her hair and placed a clip in her fringe to hold it off her face. There was nothing she hated more than getting too hot and her hair sticking to her forehead, she considered it best to deal with it beforehand. She carried her boots downstairs and sat on the bottom step to put them on. She could hear Georgie washing up and figured that she was faster at getting ready then her.

"Ta da!" Daisy swooped into the room, arms outstretched to show off her final look. She spun around for effect, laughing as she did. "What do you think?"

"Wow! You look stunning," answered Stephan. *Shit!* She thought he had left, if this was how the night was going to continue, one embarrassment after another, then Daisy would go to bed now and carry on reading the book.

"Oh, erm, thank you." Was all she could muster.

"You look a zillion dollars." He was grinning from ear to ear and was most definitely checking her out. "By the way," he continued as he turned to finish washing up, "I was complimenting your dancing earlier, I was worried you thought I was taking the mickey, that was not my intention. I was saying to Aunt Georgie how it was refreshing to see people step out and enjoy themselves at a party, instead of standing around the edges looking uncomfortable."

"Oh, well that was kind of you to say. To be honest I felt I had made a fool out of myself, but as long as it came across as having fun, that's good to know." She smiled appreciatively at him. She reached for the tea towel.

"Come on, you can't get yourself all glammed up just to dry-up it can drip-dry."

"I'm ok, I'm happy to help, gives me something to do while I wait." She was still blushing at his compliment. So as to take the heat off her she asked about him.

"Me? Well I'm aspiring artist, as is every other person in the city, that's if they are not a writer." His smile was breath-taking, "I work as a barman, waiter, whatever to pay the bills but I'm at my happiest when I'm sketching."

"Cool. What kind of things do you draw?"

"Anything really, I tend to just take photos on my phone if something captures my eye, that way I can hold the image until I get a chance to draw it, much better than trying to remember."

"So do you sell you work?"

"Yea I have a few pieces up in a gallery on Steep Hill and a few other pieces have been displayed here and there. Mostly it is friends of friends who commission me to do something in particular."

"I'd love to see what you do, I love art. I'm not an expert of anything but a beautiful picture can stir up emotions in you. That is when I would buy a canvas, not just because someone famous once did it and everyone claimed they were good. A lot of the time I don't like the mainstream stuff."

"I visited the Tate gallery the other weekend while I was down there. That was an amazing experience, the difference in the types of art displayed are immense. It was a soulful event for me. Now that is somewhere I would love to display my work. Then I would know I had made it in the art world!" The dreamy, faraway look in his eyes showed true passion for his work, *a rare commodity these days*, thought Daisy. She stacked the clean crockery on the side and they chatted as they cleared the dishes. *It was strange how with some people, such as his aunt, you just click*. The awkwardness of his appearance had passed and they were now at ease in each other's company.

Georgie floated into the kitchen, a sea of white. She looked youthful and excited. They both smiled and complimented her. The shoes went perfectly with the cream trousers and white top that she had purchased. She practised her dancing moves and they all joined in and giggled away.

"Right lets order a taxi!" Georgie exclaimed, "I'm ready to hit the town."

"Do you want me to give you a lift? I'm heading home now."

"That would be handy, if you don't mind."

"Not at all, my pleasure."

After a last minute of faffing, they were ready to go.

"Your carriage awaits," announced Stephan. He led them to his old Nissan Micra, and helped them in, holding the front seat back as Daisy climbed inelegantly into the back. After a nifty manoeuvre involving much revving and reversing, uphill starts and cursing, they were away. It was nine thirty so they were well in time for free entry, another bonus.

Chapter Fifteen- Dancing Queens

Stephan seemed surprised at their choice of club and offered to escort them elsewhere if they preferred, but Georgie told him that it had been recommended to them. He gave an odd look that Daisy couldn't quite read, and helped them out of the car.

"If you need a lift later, just let me know, I'm popping to see Tom so I'll only be up the road." Daisy and Georgie burst out laughing and hooked arms as they waved him off. "Say hi to Tom for me," Georgie shouted to the departing car. They were laughing so hard they had to wait to walk to the door of the club.

Surprisingly, given their raucous behaviour, the bouncer greeted them and opened the door for them. "Enjoy your evening."

"Thank you," they chimed, still giggling to themselves.

The heat of the place hit them, Daisy was glad she had pinned her hair back. The place was quite busy and although it was smaller than either of them had expected everyone seemed to be thoroughly enjoying themselves. They ordered drinks, they wanted to make the most of being out so decided that more cocktails would probably not be a good idea, they'd be drunk within the hour and the night would be wasted.

They managed to find an unoccupied table just off of the dance floor and sat watching the crowd dance and whoop as they sipped their drinks.

"This is great," shouted Georgie above the music.

"It is," Daisy agreed.

They were bopping away in their seats; the waitress had been right- the atmosphere in here was thrilling and the music was fantastic.

"It feels good to be out," Georgie said. She looked so happy Daisy leant over and hugged her.

"It really does."

An hour or so later the place was heaving, a lot of the men had removed their tops and were dancing frantically. Both of them were enjoying the view and decided that it was time to join in. They propped their handbags against the DJ set and set to enjoying the night. Daisy noticed that there were a lot of very glamorous older ladies in here, their outfits were divine. She felt quite underdressed next to them. The fit men danced around them and Daisy considered it unusual for young men to be interested in older ladies. Most clubs she had been to were full of young girls and leery old men. This made a nice change.

Surprisingly her feet were not aching in her new boots and her leg muscles had loosened, either that or she was immune to the pain due to the excessive alcohol consumption. Whichever it was Daisy didn't care, she danced her little heart out, pure 'no one is watching' kind of dancing. Georgie did the same and they laughed and mimicked each other at times. It was exhilarating. It was the sort of night out that, as you prepared to go out, you hoped you had when you were younger. Yet, as a young person Daisy had been, as most are, too self-conscious to fully 'let go', more than that, to just be herself. Here in a sea of people she did not know, in a city she had never been to, she didn't care.

It hadn't particularly crossed her mind to care. Daisy wished she could be like this all the time; free from self-doubt and always thinking people were viewing her negatively. Yet, as Stephan had pointed out, to be the one who jumps up and has a good time and a laugh, you look far more beautiful than the ones who have dressed up but don't do anything other than stand there looking concerned for how they look. Daisy laughed, a big hearty, contagious laugh. People around joined in and the whole crowd danced with more expression and vigour. It was so enlivening, all these people dancing wildly, no judgement or criticism because they were too busy feeling the music and going with it.

Daisy turned mid-move and there watching her from the bar was Stephan. He waved and smiled. She smiled and carried on dancing. He had obviously come along to check on the well-being of his Aunt. Yet, his Aunt was drunkenly dancing with the rest of them. Daisy signalled to her that he was here and she waved wildly at him, beckoning him over to join them. He walked over and Daisy was proud to see that he whole-heartedly adhered to the no-holes-barred rule. He danced with Georgie and then with Daisy. It was great how everyone in here danced with everyone. It was not grouped-off like in other places, people only dancing with people they knew. A young topless lad cleared a space so he could spin on the pole. After many other attempts by others, it was fantastic to see someone who knew what they were doing on there. Everyone bopped around him, safely back from his flailing legs, clapping and cheering him. He spun around, upside-down, legs out in the splits and all kinds of moves that could have done any other person a huge amount of damage.

Daisy needed to take a break, she was boiling. Georgie stayed dancing, she said she was having far too much fun to leave the dance floor. Stephan escorted her out to the garden area, or smoking area as it was. He seated her at a table and popped back in to get her a drink, this was becoming a habit for him. Two young ladies approached her table and asked if they could join her. "Sure," slurred Daisy, as she mopped her brow with a tissue.

"Are you having a good night?" said the short haired lady.

"Yes, very much so thank you." She realised she was still bopping in her seat.

"I haven't seen you here before, are you local?" asked the lady with piercings in her eyebrow and nose, and numerous differing ear-rings in her ears.

"No, I'm from Norfolk, I'm just visiting with my friend, Georgie, that's her there," Daisy pointed through the windows to where Georgie was dancing manically, surrounded by a group of tasty looking men, all of whom were worshiping her. *They really were into the older glamorous ladies here.*

The girls were extremely friendly and very tactile. They complimented her hair and her jewellery, they loved her outfit, hair, boots. With every compliment came a touch or a stroke. *This place was so friendly.* The alcohol was soaking into her system, the music was thumping through her ears. She could see Georgie dancing away. She smiled to herself and the friendly ladies.

Stephan appeared with her drink and eyed the ladies who were now sitting either side of her.

"Excuse me ladies."

The ladies moved, throwing him a disapproving look and chatted amongst themselves.

"So, how you doing?" Stephan asked Daisy, glancing at the ladies.

"Yea, I'm doing good," she slurred, "I love this place," she gestured widely, nearly tipping herself backwards.

He caught her just in time, he smiled, "I'm glad."

She carried on bopping and drinking then suddenly a thought hit her, she gasped, "I thought you were at Tom's." Hysterical giggling followed.

He raised an eyebrow, as though to question her amusement, obviously the alcohol was taking effect.

The doors flew open and out danced Georgie, a topless man on each arm. Daisy ran over and hugged her, the men did not detach, they just joined in. Georgie was having the time of her life.

"Isn't this place fabulous!" she shouted, obviously still deafened from the music.

Georgie slumped down on the nearest bench, the picnic table nearly left the ground with the force. Georgie steadied herself, laughing and holding on to the bench for dear life. Daisy and Stephan sat on the other side to equally distribute the weight. Stephan looked completely bemused by his Aunt's behaviour, Daisy was loving seeing her so happy, she really was thoroughly enjoying herself.

Her two chaperons had wandered off and were dancing together over the other side of the walled garden area. Daisy thought it was a refreshing change to see men dancing, they normally just propped up the bar and ogled the women who were dancing. Stephan placed his hand on her back.

"You ok?" She had been swaying quite precariously.

She flinched slightly; no one had paid her that kind of attention in a long time. That one gesture made her feel quite emotional again. Daisy considered touch, a strange thing, she believed it to be one of the physiological needs of humans, love and affection were such powerful yet simple things.

"Yes, thank you," she answered, her voice catching in her throat.

His touch was momentary, to steady her and get her attention more than anything else, but it had been nice, comforting somehow. The chill of the evening caught up with her and she shivered.

"It's freezing, shall we go back in?" Daisy downed her drink and informed Georgie of their plans.

"I'll join you, I need to dance."

Georgie skipped and sang as she made her way back through the doors which Stephan and Daisy held open for her.

"These shoes were made for dancing… and that's just what they'll do… la la la la la…" Daisy and Stephan looked at each other and smirked, as they followed her, closing the doors behind them.

Chapter Sixteen- Wilting Daisy

Waking up with a hangover was becoming a bad habit for Daisy. Every muscle in her body ached, her throat hurt and the brightness of the sun through the curtain was stinging her eyes. All these ailments aside, she felt elated, as though a huge weight had been lifted. Dancing and singing really was cathartic. She stretched contently and smiled, then she winced and pulled the duvet back up over her head to shield her from the sun.

At around eleven o'clock the two friends arrived in the kitchen, both in search of coffee and painkillers. They looked like the walking dead on the outside but on the inside they were cheerful and full of optimism. They worked together in unison to prepare the drinks, neither one of them could have achieved it alone this morning.

Curled up on either end of the sofa they drunk their coffee slowly and carefully, not so much to savour the experience but to save them from too much exertion. They both flinched at the sound of the doorbell. Georgie hauled herself out of the sofa.

"Good morning ladies," there was the sound of cheek kissing, "I bring sustenance!"

In glided Stephan, three coffees in a cardboard holder and a white paper bag. Taking one look at them his smile faded and he swiftly exited the room. Georgie sat herself back down and tucked her legs beneath them. Her head hit the cushion heavily.

"My oh my, we are a sight for sore eyes, aren't we?" declared Stephan as he re-entered the room with the coffees and an array of pastries on a plate. Both the women gave him a look of disdain for his comment but thanked him for the delivery of breakfast. He served each of them in turn, asking them to choose their preferred pastry. Georgie went for the croissant, Daisy the chocolate filled version she could never remember the name of. She just nodded as he pointed, Stephan had a Danish pastry. They were just what the doctor ordered, plus the painkillers were probably kicking in about now. They were starting to feel slightly more human.

"So did you have a good night?"

"It was wonderful, the people were all so friendly. I haven't danced or laughed so much in years," Georgie replied, her eyes now glinting at the memories.

"Totally," agreed Daisy, "It really was fantastic."

Stephan looked pleased that they had enjoyed themselves, but he had a mischievous look in his eye, "but…" urged Daisy, smirking at him.

"But, what?"

"You were going to say something, what was it?"

"Well nothing really." He took a huge bite out of another Danish so he couldn't speak.

Daisy eyeballed him until he relented. He really didn't understand how much pain that had caused her raw eyes. She blinked a couple of times to refresh them.

"Well I was just wondering if you realised…" a nibble of pastry.

"What?" the two women asked simultaneously.

"Seriously you must have noticed…" another bite.

"What?"

"Stephan," Georgie put on her 'Aunt' tone, "what did we not know?"

"Well, how can I put it?" he paused again for effect, Daisy got the impression he was enjoying this, "That it was a gay club!"

"What!" Daisy nearly spat her coffee all over the carpet and Georgie's hand shot to her mouth.

"Are you two joking? You must have known." He had the biggest grin on his face.

"If we had known, young man," the 'Aunt' tone again, "would we be so surprised?"

"Well I guess not. I did wonder, that's why I asked if you would have preferred to go somewhere else."

"Well gay or not, I had the best night out I can remember and in all fairness the people there were much better fun than most clubs. I didn't feel uncomfortable or leered at all evening, most refreshing if you ask me," retorted Daisy.

"Exactly," confirmed Georgie.

"Oh don't get me wrong. I wasn't being homophobic, I was just wondering how you found out about the place to be honest. A few of my friends go there and they love it." He looked worried that they thought he was insulting their new friends. "Seriously, it was great to see the fun you were having."

"Oh right," both women sat back in their seats and relaxed from their defensive stances.

"Erm, it was that young waitress in that pub that said about it, wasn't it Daisy?"

"Yep, we asked… oh God," Daisy covered her mouth with her hand, you don't think she thought we were… no?" She burst out laughing.

Georgie followed suit. "It was probably the bag on the table that gave that impression." Georgie was holding her stomach, she was laughing so hard. "If only I was so lucky to have such a glamorous girlfriend!"

"Or me," mumbled Stephan. Daisy heard him and blushed but Georgie was laughing far too hard to have heard anything. She was wiping the tears from her cheeks.

"Oh, how funny, bless her heart. Well either way, fab club."

Georgie contently sipped her coffee, Daisy was still a tad shocked by Stephan's comment, *maybe he just meant in-general, not specifically her. Yea, that was probably it,* Daisy tried to convince herself. *He was all of about twenty-five, far too young for her, and more to the point, she was too old for him.*

Daisy self-consciously pulled her cardigan tighter around her. She really felt fragile. Although she had managed to dodge her reflection so far today, she doubted she was even vaguely on the glamorous scale. But if Georgie viewed her as such through her beer-goggles then she would accept it.

"Is it ok if I grab a quick shower Georgie?"

"Of course honey, use whatever you need."

"Cheers, see you in a bit. I feel the need to humanise myself. By the way, thank you for breakfast Stephan." She gave a grateful smile.

Daisy was usually someone who liked to sing a little bit in the shower, it helped perk her up for the day ahead. It also informed the children that she was in the bathroom, as there was no lock on the door. But she felt shy to sing in someone else's house, so she just hummed slightly. She wasn't even sure what tune it was supposed to be but it helped clear her muggy head. By the time she was dried and dressed she was restored. She tied back her hair so it didn't make the back of her top wet and clipped her fringe up out of her eyes, she hadn't realised how long it had got.

Daisy was slightly put out to find that Stephan had already left by the time she came back downstairs. She was sure that he was still there when she had nipped swiftly up the stairs only minutes beforehand. Georgie told her that he had said to tell her that it was nice to meet her properly and that he wished her a safe journey home.

"Bless him, that was kind. Tell him likewise, he is a lovely young man."

"I will, he is a good lad really," Georgie agreed absently as she pottered around the kitchen in her dressing gown, "although I guess at nearly thirty, he hardly fits in the 'lad' category anymore. To me he is still a little nipper." She smiled at the memory of years having passed so fast.

"Well talking of safe journeys I best head off."

"Oh, that's a shame. We didn't get to venture up Steep Hill. Next time," she vowed.

"Definitely. I'll just grab my bags together. Oh cheeky question," Georgie turned to face her, "Could I possibly borrow one of your books?"

Georgie chuckled, "I did wonder what on earth you were going to ask, of course you can my dear. I thought for a dreaded moment you wanted Tom to escort you home." She laughed long and hard.

Daisy couldn't help but blush and laugh along. *Good old Tom.*

Chapter Seventeen- Good to be Home

Daisy had felt sad leaving Lincoln and Georgie in particular. She was so lovely and Daisy had surprised herself at how much fun she was capable of having. She had become somewhat of a recluse in the final years of her marriage to Joel. Not because he enforced so much as through sheer tiredness from running around after the children all day and neither her nor Joel having the energy to socialise. *It was a shame really,* thought Daisy, *that the fun tends to edge out of marriages over time. Her and Joel had been quite the socialites in the beginning of their relationship. But she guessed that it was not just them who got busy, all of their friends had.*

Her friendship with Georgie had somewhat spurred her along into building up a new social life for herself, and it may help the children if her friends had children of their own. The last thing she wanted at this stage in her life was to start dating or venture into a new relationship. She had a lot of work to do on herself before then. She wanted to enjoy herself as a person in her own right, not just as part of a couple.

Daisy allowed herself the luxury of a quick afternoon nap. Feeling more refreshed she set to cleaning through the house, hoovering and changing bedsheets ready for the children's return. She had missed them terribly and maybe another time she would take them with her. They would love to climb Steep Hill and explore the castle. Georgie had offered the other spare room if they wanted to come, although she had expressed prior warning as it was currently the junk room.

It must be odd, considered Daisy, *to live alone after raising a family and being married, she admired Georgie's strength. She was not sure she would fare as well. Although, all things considered she had to admit that her and the children were adapting fast to life without Joel. Plus, she guessed it was a slow transition as the children grew up. Hmm. She pulled her mind back to the here and now. She would construct a plan of action.* She loved lists; her new mission to find a social life seemed like a good a reason as any.

Seated at the kitchen table with a fresh coffee and a sparkling house around her, Daisy started her list.

1. Make new friends
2. Join groups
3. ~~Get a dog~~ become a dogwalker
4. Look for a part-time job
5. Consider an evening course

So far so good. Not set in stone, the dog might not be such a good idea, taking it fir walks would mean that she would get out and about; but then there would be the poo. The company would be nice, but still there would be hair. Ok, maybe a dogwalker, that would cross two things off her list; part-time job and getting a dog. Oh, actually three, as she would make friends with the owners and fellow dogwalkers. She was liking this idea more and more. *This is why lists were great. Dogwalkers are kind of a group or have groups, didn't they? And maybe, just to round off, they might meet in the evenings or weekends. Sorted.*

She sat back with a sigh of contentment. *Tomorrow, once the children were at school she would make up some leaflets to hand around and post through every house in the village. She might not make her fortune but she would achieve her goals.* She reached for her coffee. It was cold. She drunk it anyway. She figured her coffee being cold showed that she was fully absorbed with the task at hand.

The doorbell ringing broke her out of her contemplation. She literally skipped to the door, unlocked it and flung it open.

"Yay! You are home!" she hugged the children to her as though she had not seen them in years.

"Mum, mum, I can't breathe," complained Sally

Cory just hugged her back, no complaints and with a similar force to hers. She welled up and it took Joel speaking to her to break her out of her overly-emotional-mother-moment.

"What, sorry I wasn't listening."

"I was just letting you know that Sally lost a tooth, it is in her pocket."

"Ah, honey," she faced her daughter, "which one?"

Sally opened wide and pointed at the gap in her incisors.

"Fabulous!" She made a mental note to inform the tooth fairy, so she could check the coinage in her purse. "We'll pop it under your pillow in a minute."

The children ran off into the house after giving their Dad big hugs. "You are looking well by the way."

"Ah thank you, that's very kind of you to say." She smoothed her clothing down. "Are things ok with you?"

"Yea, not bad actually. I've started dating again," he stage whispered, "it's scary out there."

They both smiled. "It is, although I was at a gay club last night and to be fair, I think you got the better dating scene." The colour ran out of Joel's face, "The men are extremely friendly. And fit" She stage whispered back.

"Really? Are you joking?" He looked almost hopeful that she was, but equally intrigued.

"No seriously, my friend, I was staying with up in Lincoln took me. It was the most fun night out ever. Highly recommended and much less intimidating than the straight scene." They laughed, she leant against the door frame. "You'll be fine Joel, good looking man such as yourself."

They hugged and he left. Strangely they got on so much better since they had resolved everything. She considered that because of the secrets that they had withheld from each other throughout their marriage they had closed parts of themselves off. Her with the fact that part of her heart and soul still belonged to Tristan and him with his lust for other men. Now that she could think of, or meet up with Tristan as and when she so wished and it in no way affected their relationship the same was true of his situation. They both wished happiness for each other, she almost envied the amount of fun he would be having in the gay scene. Yet she was now a single mother who walked people's dogs for them in order to have a social life. When she thought of it that way it was hard not to become disheartened. But Daisy was still too elated from her weekend and her new plan. He beeped as he drove off and she waved.

"What's this?" asked the Cory as she rounded the corner of the kitchen. She had to think what they could be referring to.

"Oh, my list? Well, that is a plan for Mummy."

"Why did you cross out the bit about getting a dog?" Puppy eyes were deployed; very apt.

"How about you get the biscuit tin, I make a cup of tea. Then you can tell me all about your weekend and I'll explain this list. Ok?"

"Ok." They answered simultaneously.

The children were having their Sunday evening bathtime. This usually resulted in them becoming cleaner and relaxed ready for bed. although the house became messier and she became more stressed. But tonight it didn't seem to bother her. It had felt really nice to have sat at the kitchen table drinking tea and dunking biscuits, while they all chatted. She guessed it was part of the transition. It seemed like only five minutes since they had sat in their highchairs decorating the kitchen with rusks. It would probably feel like only five minutes having passed when they would be adults sat at the kitchen table on visits home while waiting for their Uni washing to be done. Just the thought was making her quite emotional.

She popped her head round the bathroom door, "You ok Cory?" A bubble-bearded boy replied a big 'yes'. Sally had finished her bath and Cory was in her topped up water. She was sat in her pyjamas arranging her teddies, chatting away to them as she did so. Daisy watched her for a second, *she had grown so fast, how was it possible she was nearly eight?*. Sally looked up and jumped.

"Mum!"

"Sorry, I was just thinking how grown up you are now, shall we go dry your hair honey?"

"Ok," she hopped up, "I'll be back in a minute," she informed her teddies.

Daisy could hear Cory singing and splashing away happily.

"Five more minutes Cory"

"Oh, but I've only been in here five seconds."

Daisy smirked and reiterated her instruction. There was a bit more whinging and then the singing recommenced. Daisy sat Sally at her dressing table. She fiddled with Daisy's jewellery box, trying on her rings and bangles. This had become part of the bathtime/bedtime routine. It was a nice way to catch up and ensure that Sally was ok, and she seemed to chat away quite happily. She told Daisy all about her Dad's new apartment and her new room and how Cory was feeling about it too. Apparently, she was worried that her brother was finding it difficult over the weekend's with their Dad. Once she had finished drying and plaiting Sally's hair, Cory padded through wrapped loosely in a towel. He looked so cute. Sally replaced all the jewellery and returned to her room to arrange her teddies.

Cory hopped up onto the stool and Daisy towel dried his hair with the corner of his bath sheet. Then she brushed and faffed it with her hands as she blow-dried it. As she did so, she chatted away in her best 'hairdresser' accent. She asked her 'client' how his day at work was, and where his was going on holiday this year, he giggled away, she asked how his family were and whether his hair looked as he wanted. Cory chuckled away to himself. They then popped into his room to fetch his pyjamas.

Moments later they were both tucked up in bed and she read the 'Nothing' book, they loved the part were grandpa recognises Nothing. After it was finished she gave them both a kiss and cuddle.

"Night, sweet dreams. Love you."

"Night." They chorused.

Daisy made herself a cup of tea and took her list, laptop and drink to bed. She was really excited about her new venture, she loaded up the laptop and experimented with differing font styles and wording. After checking her Facebook, and cringing at all the photos she had been tagged in from the reunion, she tried again with her leaflet. She settled with her initial idea which worked best, as ever with these things. She decided that simple was best, a picture of a dog, her contact details and pricing. That was the hardest part to finalise. She was unsure whether to charge one rate or by size of dog. She decided on a set rate, otherwise it would all get too complicated. She could envision having to weigh each dog before agreeing to a price. In her tired state she considered charging by the amount of poo each dog produced, she smirked at the concept.

Just as she was closing up for the night a friend request popped up. From Stephan.

Chapter Eighteen- Snap, Crackle and Pop

It probably would have been more sensible to have rejected it or ignored it. Yet, Daisy was feeling elated from her weekend and planning her new enterprise. Also, she was curious. *Possibly not the best idea but how else was she going to spend her evening now the children were asleep?* She started off scrolling through his photos, he really was angelic and extremely devilish all in one fine specimen. Now she knew he was closer in age than she had previously thought, it didn't seem so wrong. Maybe she could tweak her moral compass on this one occasion. There were varying pictures of him out with friends, a couple with Georgie at a family event, and old childhood pictures. She thought it was unusual that there were not many of him with girlfriends, although she rationalised that he was probably a private sort of chap who didn't advertise to all and sundry his relationship status or his food consumption.

Just as she was considering logging off, a personal message popped up.

'Hope you don't mind me adding you, I thought it would be nice to keep in touch.'

She gasped, smiled and blushed all in one swift movement. *Since when had she been such a girl about chatting to men?* However, he was on a slightly different scale to the Dads at the school or the man in the shop.

'Don't mind at all, nice to hear from you.' Send. *Ahh.* She found herself wringing out her hands and staring manically at the screen, awaiting his reply.

'Figure you got home safe. Aunt Georgie rang me after you left to tell me what a wonderful time the two of you had. To be honest I think it is great that she has you as a friend. She gets quite lonely, no matter how she comes across. It was so nice to see her having such fun.'

She felt choked up by his openness and also she felt the same towards Georgie. 'That is kind of you to say, she really is a fabulous lady and I'm so grateful to her. I needed the break from home and she has been so kind to me.' She read back her reply as she awaited his, and wondered if it came across as sad and desperate. Well she guessed she was; admitting it, especially to a man she hardly knew.

'Do you feel better now though?'

'Much. Thanks for brunch by the way, you'd gone before I got to say it.'

'No worries. I dropped you off remember, I knew you'd need it. Lol.' He added a winking smiley.

'I had drunk a lot. He he.'

Their conversation flitted from jobs to family, to social lives, or in her case the recent discovery of one.

'I have to admit,' he wrote, 'that I have looked through your photos.' *So it wasn't just her.* She was suddenly flicking through them all in her mind and remembered the recently tagged reunion photos, but then recalled that he had been at the event so seen her in full swing.

'Oh God.' Was her simple reply.

'What? You look wonderful and you have a really nice family, you all look so happy. How long have you been married?' *What? He had complimented her again… and why did he think she was married?*

'Thank you and I'm no longer married, we divorced earlier this year.'

'Sorry. I didn't mean to pry, it was just there was one of you with two children and a man, who I assumed was your husband.'

'Oh, I know the one you mean, that is my ex-husband, we were at a christening, we still get on.'

'That makes sense then, great that you still get on.'

'Yea, easier on the children.'

'I bet.'

He was quite tactful after that and didn't question her further but instead chatted about the last christening that he'd attended and how the baby threw up on his suit and he'd spent the rest of the night smelling of puke. He had not dared to ask anyone to dance, after that and had been saved by Georgie, who danced the night away with him. Daisy could envisage the pair of them, him whiffing of baby sick and Georgie raving away the evening as she had last night. The thought made Daisy smile. She was thoroughly enjoying their interaction. It was far easier to talk to him without having to face him.

'So when are you over next?'

'No idea, to be honest, I have promised the children that I will take them up to see the castle. They are very excited.'

'Fabulous, you will have to let me know when you are coming up. It will be great to see you again.'

'Totally. I'm gonna head off now, kids to get up for in the morning. Great talking to you.'

'Take care of yourself, night.'

'Night.'

Having closed her laptop she slid down in the bed and snuggled the duvet around her. For the first time since she had moved into the house she felt, happy, content and a tad giggly as she drifted off to sleep. Stephan was an unexpected friend to have made. It was crazy how sometimes while you are busy looking for one thing, which you believe you want, something else comes along, which is strangely better suited to you and your situation. Serendipity at its best.

As she got comfy and sleepier she replayed the events involving Stephan in her mind. She smiled to herself at the remembrance of him supplying her with cocktails and protection from Tristan. He had looked after her in the club and saved her from the 'obviously now' lesbians. But the part that stood out most to her was the way he had supplied brunch for her and his aunt after playing designated driver/bodyguard the evening before. Finally, sleep caught up with her and she embraced it with visions of Stephan to fill her dreams.

Seemingly, ten minutes later the kids woke her up with a start. They were loudly requesting that she solved the argument about who got the last Weetabix, something to do with Cory having too many yesterday and how he always got them. Daisy had no idea or inclination as to how to deal with this. According to her mobile she had actually had seven hours sleep, she certainly did not feel as though she had. She asked them to wait a second, and she gradually edged her way out of bed, one unwilling limb at a time.

She could still hear the war continuing while she was in the bathroom. *Here we go, one of those days.* She smiled at her reflection as she washed her hands and splashed water on her face. 'I'll handle it,' she chanted to her smiley alter ego in the mirror; she smiled back and entered the kitchen ready for anything!

She was not, however, prepared for this!

It transpired that, if the children had not started bickering; thus shouting, then arguing, then throwing handfuls of differing breakfast cereals at each other, many of the following events would not have happened.

Firstly, there would have been enough cereal for everyone. Two, Sally would not have needed a shower before school. Thirdly, subsequently there would have been enough milk. Fourth, Cory would not have nearly killed his sister because she claimed that rice crispies still go snap, crackle and pop even if they are in his hair. Five, Daisy would not have grounded them, forever, needed a shower herself due to entering the kitchen at the wrong moment, and she would not have found out the rice crispies still snapped, crackled and popped an hour after they touch milk. She also wouldn't be stood here, exhausted and deflated and in utter despair, trying to decide on the 'safest' cereal to purchase just as Tristan walked down aisle three of Tesco!

Chapter Nineteen- Sod's Law

The urge to run and hide was so strong that Daisy almost felt herself hold her feet in position. Why was it that she never bumped into anyone she knew when she had made an effort, the same as no one visited if she'd cleaned the house, only ever after it had been destroyed.

"Wow, morning Daisy, how you doing?"

"Great," she plastered on her best fake smile.

Obviously, as ever these scenes play out in the movies, he was looking impeccable to the point that Daisy had the urge to start her own food fight. *God, she really was in a weird mood today*. How anyone could seriously look that good at nine thirty on a Monday morning she had no idea. Maybe the stud that he was, this was him on his way home after a wild weekend. Evidently, in reality he was grabbing some essential items ready for his trip back home.

"I'm back to work tomorrow and I figured it was easier to get some supplies this end so that after the drive I can just relax with a coffee. Speaking of which did you want to join me for a coffee before I set off?" *He was smooth,* too smooth, as Daisy found herself agreeing to meet him in the café after she had finished shopping.

Tristan laughed heartily as she relayed the events of the weekend and this morning's war. Daisy found herself calming down and enjoying his company. To think that he had been her reason for needing to escape seemed ridiculous now. Just as she was wiping the cappuccino froth from her top lip, he leant forward meaningfully. Daisy froze, she knew that look.

"Why did you run off the other day? Did I do or say something wrong?"

"No, not really, it was just a tad more honesty than I'm used to dealing with." She figured to brush off his deep and meaningful questioning was safer. Tesco's café was probably not the best location for matters of the heart. Especially ones which held such raw emotions.

"Oh, ok." He looked deflated, that was obviously not the answer he had been looking for. "Can I be honest with you, again." He gave a weary smile.

"Sure, but can I warn you that I am not necessarily in the best frame of mind to deal with such things, I try to wait until at least Wednesday." She smiled, what she hoped was a light-hearted one, aiming to soften the seriousness with humour, her best defence.

He smiled back but continued, "it was just that after the other day I felt as though I had opened up too much to you, too soon after being back in contact, but I had held those feelings in for so many years and seeing you again just brought them flooding back and it was as though I was no longer in control." He ran his fingers through his hair, "How can I put this… it was as if you were a magnet for all those emotions and they just threw themselves at you, like I wasn't in control of them. Does that sound ridiculous?"

"Strangely no." She considered how she had felt, how she had cried her way home and sobbed for Britain on her arrival, then fled for Lincoln at the first opportunity. She understood.

He was looking extremely uncomfortable yet a glimmer of hope shone from his eyes as he watched her.

"Honestly," she blurted, "It broke my heart to know that you had felt so strongly for me but spent a lifetime avoiding it. We were so happy, all those years ago and that one thing happened," she cleared her throat, "and you just left, deserted me, at the point I needed you most."

He hung his head, she was unsure as to whether he was about to cry. As he slowly raised his head again, he looked her straight in the eyes and said what she had needed to hear, "Sorry."

It took all of her composure not to burst in to tears or lean over and hug him and the two of them could cry it out together. But she sat strong, "I know." Was the only reply she could muster.

They drank their coffees in silence and then he announced that he had best leave. She stood to leave also, fetching her bag from beside the chair.

"Daisy?" she turned back to face him.

"Yes?" Her heart had stopped beating, the sound of it paused so that she could listen to whatever it was he was about to say. Her mouth went dry and she clung to her bag like a life jacket.

"Thank you."

"What for?"

"Still having anything to do with me, I know that I hurt you beyond compare and I have lived with the regret all this time. I'm not asking for forgiveness, as I know that I don't deserve it. But are we ok to stay friends please?" He had tears in his eyes, and the night he had left played through her mind. She took a deep breath.

"Tristan, I know that losing that baby was harsh, but it was not entirely your fault."

He looked at her almost disbelievingly. Not only had she said it aloud but she no longer seemed to hold a grudge. He appeared to have had the weight of the world removed from him in that instant.

They hugged and it was all either of them could do to hold the emotions back. Instead they fetched their shopping from the trolley locker and slowly wandered towards their cars. As they arrived at Daisy's Tristan remarked, "You are looking well by the way."

"Am I? Thank you."

This was becoming a common compliment, maybe there was some truth in it? They hugged one more time and Daisy packed her shopping into the boot, watching him walk over to his car on the far side of the carpark. She wanted to call out to him to come back or follow him, hug him and never let go. She had never felt as safe in the arms of anyone as much as she did Tristan. They knew each other so well, maybe too well. They had grown into adults together and been in awe of each other's strength of character as they had dealt with life.

Chapter Twenty- Living With Regret

Losing the baby had been the breaking point of their relationship, neither one of them wanted to face up to the reality of the situation. They had still been young, twenty-one, but it had seemed so right when they had found out. In the beginning, they had kept it a secret from people but as the weeks went by people noticed her pale complexion and her fragile movements. She was sick from the word go, practically the second the egg was fertilised. But they had been tested and scanned and everything was well, but Daisy felt as though something was wrong.

Only ten weeks into the pregnancy, as word was spreading through their friends and family circle, Daisy had passed out unexpectantly at work. By the time they had got her to the hospital she was conscious but in extortionate pain. Tristan was away at the time, she couldn't even remember where he had been, his grandparents or something. Her Mum had met the ambulance as it arrived and stayed with her throughout. Two and a half hours later she had miscarried. The consultants and nurses had reassured her than she would have no lasting damage and there was no reason that she couldn't go on to have healthy pregnancies in the future.

Daisy hardly heard what they were saying. She was heartbroken, their tiny baby was gone. They had planned everything, listed items to buy, started making the spare room of their apartment into a nursery. Argued over names. But now it was all gone. Daisy's Mum had rung Tristan and he was already on his way to the train station, heading for home. But he was too late.

Her Mum had offered to stay with her at the apartment, but Daisy just shook her head and whispered that she just wanted to go home. It was dark by the time they pulled up in front of the building. Daisy looked up at it with apprehension and fear but also a longing to be in her own space, surrounded by her own things. She calmly thanked her Mum, hugged her and let herself out of the car. She hadn't turned on any other light than the hallway one.

Tristan arrive home at 3.15am, he found Daisy in the nursery, in the dark, curled up hugging one of the teddies they had bought. He stood staring at her for a moment and then the strength that had propelled him home gave way and he dropped to his knees beside her, tears streaming from his eyes. Daisy opened her eyes, at the sudden noise, they were wide and fearful. He scooped her up, teddy and all and as gently as he could carried her to their room. He removed her shoes and brushed her hair out of her face, where it had stuck to her tearstained cheeks, and tucked the duvet around her tiny frame. She had somehow looked smaller. So vulnerable. So lost. Tristan had gently laid down next to her, cuddling her and the teddy. The pair of them had cried themselves to sleep, the bear had soaked up the tears the pillows had missed.

The following few weeks had been difficult. Daisy didn't want to talk about it or even acknowledge that there had ever been a baby. Tristan, her Mum, his Mum, had all tried to talk to her, get her to open up, but she had shut down. Three days after the miscarriage he had come home to find all the little baby items, and the cot a friend had let them borrow, out by the bins in the carpark. The teddy had caught his eye first and he had salvaged it before storming up the stairs to find out what was going on.

Daisy was in the nursery, manically stripping wallpaper, the music was on loud and she was still wearing the clothes she had arrived home in, all those days ago. When he confronted her, she had shouted at him that 'had we not bought things before three months, we would have been ok, he would still be here with us.

Stupid bloody baby stuff. I hate it, I hate this room, I hate you.' Tristan was unsure how best to deal with her.

She from silence to this and it became hard to know how to judge her each day. She hardly washed or changed her clothes, she took no pride in anything anymore. She had quit her job, even though they had offered her sick pay. Whatever had been left intact after the baby, she broke, figuratively out of spite and anger at the injustice of the situation.

Tristan found himself staying later at work to avoid her, he would go for a drink with the lads or pop to his Mum's for tea and sympathy. Daisy had lost more than the baby, she had lost herself. For all the best intentions, Tristan could not cope. Every part of their life, their relationship, their future had been blown apart. He wanted to acknowledge their loss, he wanted to talk about it, he wanted to place the scan picture on the shelf with the teddy and remember. Instead the teddy was tucked at the back of his boot of his car, behind his toolbox, in case she saw it and tried to throw it away.

Six months later Daisy was feeling better. She was working again, they had let her have her job back. She was thankfully putting on weight again; she had become so desperately thin afterwards, now she was getting back to normal. But Tristan could not seem to connect with her anymore or her with him. A divide had come between them and it seemed that it was becoming an unfixable void. They had eventually decided that enough was enough and they parted. The final part of both their hearts had broken at that moment, yet neither one of them was strong enough to hold on any longer. Tristan had moved away and Daisy had moved back closer to her Mum. Every day he awoke, wishing he had been stronger or got home quicker. Every day he missed Daisy. The teddy had travelled with Tristan and lived in a box in his wardrobe ever since. Daisy and the baby had stayed living in his heart and soul.

Twenty-one- Closed Daisy

Bizarrely Daisy did not feel so upset by their meeting as she had previously done. The acknowledgement of the circumstance under which they had separated had somehow cleared the air. The elephant in the room had finally become the topic of conversation. Indirectly, of course, but still confronted. After packing away the shopping Daisy had loaded up the laptop, she still had a couple of hours until the schoolrun. Between scrolling down her Facebook wall and pottering about doing housework, Daisy considered the best way to market her new venture. She needed money and her brain needed a change of subject. She decided to put up a status and see if she got any advice or customers, you never know. Her friends were always putting up statuses about their dogs and how much they had grown.

Daisy printed out a handful of leaflets that she had prepared the night before and tried to push the running commentary of fears to one side long enough to hand them out at the school. She considered whether it would be better to ask to pop them in the book folders, that way she would catch more of the demographic she was aiming for, and there was more chance that the parents who worked, and probable needed her services would get in touch. Her stomach was in knots, but she tried to convince herself that it was excitement rather than fear.

She started a list of things she would need including dog treats, poo bags, and anti-bacterial hand-sanitiser. Her stomach was now turning out of aversion for the notion of this profession. But she took a deep breath and considered the fact that between the two children she had changed many a dirty nappy, she could handle it. Bundling her pile of leaflets into her handbag she headed off to the school. Why was she so nervous, ultimately she was offering a service, to help people?

Maybe she was more of an employee than a go-it-alone entrepreneur.

Thankfully for Daisy her two best playground friends were sneaking a cigarette behind the overgrown nature garden. She skipped over and hid with them, even though she wasn't smoking. They greeted each other and Emily asked her how she was. Daisy regaled the fabulous weekend she had had and Sarah and Emily laughed at the story about gay clubbing, and ohed and ahed at the thought of Stephan. They also liked the idea of the dog walking. Instantly she had her first two clients. Neither of them could afford to pay her more than one day a week but she was grateful for the support and also considered it helpful for people just to see her walking the dogs. She felt a t-shirt design might be her next project, maybe even little dog jackets with her logo on it. She felt more enthused now that she had gotten a good reaction from people. She didn't care if they were just being nice. Nice would do right now. Handing the leaflets around the school playground was not as difficult as she had made it in her mind. She was surprised to receive really good feedback.

❀

Her services were becoming popular, she had gone from having 'pity' clients, to having five main ones. Although she was finding it physically challenging, it was somehow exhilarating to be walking for six miles a day. She could see the difference in her attitude and general outlook on life. She was even smiling, without alcohol! Her children begged her to wait until after school to walk the dogs so they could join in. Daisy was so pleased that not only did the children seem to think it was a good idea but also that they wanted to help. As it turned out, the children had a plan. Some of the other children in the village decided that as Daisy was going to the park that she could take them too.

After much explaining to both children and parents, she had settled on the fact that obviously she would keep an eye on them if she saw them but in no way could she take a professional stance if anything happened, her liability insurance covered dog-related issues not children.. But it transpired over the following weeks that Daisy had children walking along chatting with her as she walked. Or taking charge of the dogs so that she wasn't being pulled along too much. She enjoyed the company and all though she didn't know much about dogs she researched online to find the best way to conduct her business.

She had to admit she had been tired out in the beginning; ok, exhausted. But as that had passed and her body and mind adjusted to her new exertion, she found that her body was toning up and her head felt less clogged up with stress and worry. Walking, chatting to people or alone, her mind seemed to process her concerns or troubles. She would suddenly gasp and exclaim something out loud, making the dogs and any unsuspecting passers by jump. On the whole she felt the best she had in years, if not, ever.

In the midst of her new venture she had cleared her mind of all the niggling concerns about money, she was making enough to get by now as many of her dogwalking clients used her as a daily service. Her worries about Tristan's return had waned, he text her every now and again but he was back home and busy, so contact was few and far between. Joel was having fun dating again and that gave Daisy peace of mind that he was ok. Her friendship with Stephan was blossoming nicely, no pressure, no particular love interest going on other than the fact he made her stutter with nerves. Georgie was liking the fact that they had become friends, she had said that it made it more of an excuse for Daisy to keep visiting.

All in all life was good. Daisy felt that she was finally bringing everything together, and even her organisational skills were improving. The children were much more content and happy. Thus she was more content and happy; or vice versa.

It was mid-June and the promise of summer was in the air. She was enjoying her job more as she had got to know her dogs' temperaments and characteristics, and which treats they preferred. The weather had improved immensely and so had the overall mood of the general population. Daisy had realised that she had a spring in her step and a smile on her face. It was Friday and it was this weekend that she had planned to take the children to Lincoln to stay with Georgie. Stephan was looking forward to catching up with her and meeting the children as well. Georgie had cleared out the spare room and made herself a few quid by having a little yard sale the previous weekend. She had informed her that with the money she had made she might pop down to Ann Summers again and get a friend for Tom. Daisy had spat out the coffee that she had been mistakenly drinking at the moment the text came through.

Daisy was really looking forward to their trip, mixed with a touch of apprehension. She had never taken the children away on holiday or much more than a trip to the library on her own, that had turned out quite disastrous, to say the least. So, taking them to Lincoln for three days made her agitated. The children had cheered when she announced the trip and then followed it with an interrogation process the FBI would be proud of. They wanted to know everything from the colour of the curtains that would be in the bedroom to when the castle had been built and why. Daisy justified these questions as healthy enthusiasm and interest. But after they had spent two hours Googling facts about Lincoln and getting her to text Georgie about whether they had to bring their own toothbrushes or did Georgie have ones at her house, like Daddy did, for them, her patience was wearing thin.

On Thursday she had started packing their belongings and writing lists of items they might forget. This 'fun' idea was turning into a military operation and Daisy was glad of her mid-day walk with two of her regular dogs to clear her head a bit. The sun was shining and the dogs were meandering along nicely. Her phone bleeped in her pocket.

'Hi, how are you' it read. A rush of panic rushed through her and as though the dogs sensed it, they stopped and looked up at her; almost awaiting her next command.

'I'm good, how are you?' she replied, her hand involuntarily shaking.

'Glad you are ok. You up for coffee?'

Erm, was she? 'Yea, can do.'

"Good," said a voice behind her.

She jumped out of her skin and the dogs reacted, turning swiftly and nearly knocking her flying. There stood Tristan, a flask in one hand and a big cheeky grin on his face. Her reaction, however, was not quite as upbeat.

"What the hell!" she exclaimed, slightly louder than he had expected. The smile dropped from his face and he looked confused and disappointed. Obviously he had thought this was a nice idea, surprise her with coffee. But Daisy did not like surprises, she liked to be organised and prepared, whether or not she ever actually achieved it was completely beside the point. She wanted to be an organised person, always in control, thus she would (in her imaginary world) be calm. He had however, knocked her off guard. There she had been strolling along the side of the play park, thinking about whether she should pack a couple of extra sets of underwear each, just in case, and then Tristan had appeared.

She considered that at least she had not been too shocked, as he had text her but at the moment he appeared she had been mulling over why he was thinking of her, what clothing she had that was clean and not packed, and could quickly race home and change into. Instead she was standing in front of him, two yapping dogs at her feet, covered in mud, sweat and looking windswept. All these things in a man's fantasy might have been sexy but Daisy was under no illusion that the reality in this case was not in the slightest bit arousing.

He had lowered the flask to his side and he was patiently waiting for her to say something.

"Quiet you two!," she snapped at the dogs, she didn't mean to be horrible to them but with all the yapping and tugging on their leads her brain was struggling to function.

"Hello." was all her scrambled brain could muster.

"Hello, sorry I didn't mean to startle you. I came to your house but your neighbour said that you had gone to walk the dogs and aimed me in this direction. Sorry." he repeated.

She made a mental note to speak to her neighbour and inform her that the next time a handsome man asked after her, please do not send him to where she had gone. Possibly a better way to deal with the situation would have been to have kept him talking, text her, then hold his attention chatting about flowers or something, so she could sneak back, clean up and be prepared.

"Well I don't know quite what to say Tristan," she knew she was wrinkling up her nose as she spoke, "It is good to see you, of course, and lovely of you to bring coffee. Very thoughtful." She was unsure whether her face was telling him the same as the words coming out of her mouth, but nevertheless he seemed to relax, and his smile returned. Equally, the dogs laid down, having decided that they were not needed to protect her against this person and also that their walk was currently postponed.

"May I walk with you?"

"Erm, yea, I guess so." Daisy was not the best at being upfront about her true feelings, instead she was polite.

After the initial awkwardness had subsided they walked along quite comfortable in each other's company. She decided that being in his company was actually nice. They chatted about how they had both been the last few weeks, what was new with them both and how well she was doing, and looking. She filled him in on her little dogwalking business and how well it was going and how the children had surprisingly settled down in the new house without Joel. He told her that work was going well but he was considering going self-employed to try to reduce his hours. His parents had both been unwell of late and so he was finding it hard living so far away and juggling work and seeing them.

"I'm considering moving back home." If her feelings had already been mixed about her trip then they were now in turmoil. On one side it would be great to have him close by, they got on well enough; she enjoyed catching up with him occasionally. But the thought that she could regularly bump into him in Tesco rather than once in a blue moon unsettled her. She might consider shopping online more. The overpowering feeling was that it would be fabulous to have Tristan 'home'. To her she felt, and had always felt, that Tristan to her was home. Her heart filled with joy and simultaneously her head warned her to be careful.

They stopped half-way around her normal route and he poured them both a coffee. The dogs laid at her feet, glad of the break. Tristan and Daisy perched on a log on the edge of a field and stared off into the distance, both of them deep in their own thoughts.

Daisy wished this was how life had turned out for them; to have spent a lifetime taking walks and sharing a flask of coffee. The all too familiar lump in her throat returned and she coughed in order to stop herself from crying.

She felt his gaze on her, "You ok? Is it the coffee?"

She laughed, "No, not at all, the coffee is surprisingly good."

"Surprisingly?" he mimicked, "Charming!" he grinned.

She laughed and mocked, "Ok, ok, it is the best coffee I have ever tasted!"

They giggled away like a couple of kids, jesting with each other, the banter between them had always been extremely witty and the two of them against others would win out every time. Daisy remembered many an evening with friends where there were tears, laughter all round and eventually people would give up trying to compete with them. When things had been good between them the chemistry had been amazing. Her and Joel had got on really well too, of course, but it had never been quite the same. She liked the fact that all these years later they still naturally sunk back into the same train of thought. It was like a comforting blanket being wrapped around her, or the pair of them. She felt her cheeks flush. If he noticed, he didn't mention it and they finished their drinks and headed back to return the dogs and then to her house.

It was an awkward moment as she was unsure whether to invite him in or not. She did but he declined, apparently he had houses and view. She too had a trip to finish packing for and children to pick up from school. The day had gone far too fast; not that she was complaining, it was much better than sitting around feeling lost and with the added bonus of seeing Tristan.

She made a calming cup of tea and allowed herself a few minutes before setting off to do the school run.

How did she actually feel about the concept of him moving back? Hmm, it was a hard one to call to be honest. As today had proved, she enjoyed his company, a lot, but to have him within 'bumping into distance', well that was a whole different matter. Not only would it mean that he might make these 'chance' visits a regular occurrence but also she would have to be 'presentable' at all times 'just in case'. Her stomach twisted and turned at the idea of the possibilities that this might bring. She didn't believe that he had any intentions of proceeding towards any kind of relationship past that of friends. She could never be too sure that this was not his intention. The vision of such a situation flashed through her mind and it did not scare her as much as she felt it should.

Chapter Twenty-Two- Assistant Required

Business was getting busy, Daisy was by no means complaining about this but she needed a helper. Considering that Facebook and handing around leaflets had helped her to find the initial clients and from there it had been word of mouth, sticking with what was best was the logical way to go. She sat at the laptop and wrote out a quick advertisement. The problem was that although she needed help she was not going to be able to pay them very well. She figured that a teenager needing a bit of pocket money or a retired person or even a parent at home, like her, might be her best hope. Basically that was quite a few options, in fact, other than the working people, it was most people in the village. An hour later, and almost in a deja vu moment, she headed off to the school, leaflets in hand. She had merged the two advertisements together in an attempt to bring in new business and hire a helper.

With dinner underway Daisy spent a few minutes on Facebook catching up with the events of everyone else's lives. She rested her feet on the chair next to her and sipped a strong coffee. She was lagging; all this walking was great exercise and mostly she felt energetic but today she felt drained. She huffed as the phone started to ring, she did not want to speak to anyone; she just wanted to sit, do nothing meaningful, other than to intermittently stir the spaghetti bolognese. Sally ran through to grab the phone just as Daisy had started lifting herself off the chair. Sally answered the phone in her best 'grown up voice'.

"Hello, what do you want?" she pulled a confused face as she listened to the reply.

"Yes my Mummy is here." She handed the phone to Daisy, "I'm sorry." Her bottom lip stuck out and with her head hanging low. She stood next to Daisy almost awaiting her doom. Daisy was concerned, *whoever could it be to make her react like that?* With one arm wrapped around her daughter's shoulders she spoke into the phone.

"Hello?"

"Hello. This is Mrs Flanagan. Don't worry this is not about the children, I needed to speak to you about a sensitive matter.

"Erm, ok, please hold on a second." The penny dropped and she realised that her daughter obviously thought that she was in trouble. The headteacher did not phone her Mum for no reason.

Daisy bent down, the phone away from her mouth, and spoke gently to Sally. "Sweetheart Mrs Flanagan said that this phone call is nothing to do with either of you, she needs to speak to Mummy, about grown up things, so you're ok, you're are not in trouble."

Sally's shoulders dropped instantaneously and her head sprung back up and she skipped off to her bedroom to finish making tea for her teddies. Daisy absently stirred the sauce as she readdressed Mrs Flanagan.

"Sorry about that, how can I help?"

"It's ok, erm, I don't know quite how to broach the subject to be honest, it is not something I am familiar with."

"Ok..." Daisy frowned, *whatever was she going on about?* if it wasn't about her children. It couldn't be her parking as she rarely drove to the school these days. She always cleaned up after dogs she walked, no matter how much it made her gag. *Oh God, it couldn't be about her liaison with Tristan could it? What business would that be of the school?* She stirred more vigorously.

"Well, it has come to my attention," she cleared her throat, "that you have been handing out leaflets at the school."

"Yes..." the sauce bubbled and spat.

"You, apparently did not ask permission to do this."

"Oh, I didn't realise that I needed it, as I asked last time and they are pretty much the same." *Why did she feel the need to justify herself?*

"I understand… however… everything that is advertised through the school needs to be checked over by both myself and a member of the diocese."

"Oh, sorry."

Mrs Flanagan coughed again, "This would not normally have been too much of a concern..." more throat clearing, "...but Vicar Dean dropped by the school this afternoon and saw one of your flyers."

"Hmm." Daisy was now stabbing at the sauce, trying to pop the bubbles before they spat at her again. She was no longer interested in what she was going on about.

"He drew it to my attention that your leaflet was inappropriate..." she left the end of the sentence hanging.

At that point Daisy chipped in, "Ok, to be honest I have absolutely no idea what it is that you are trying to say. In future I will check with you before handing them out and I am sorry, I really do have to go though as we are about to have dinner." That excuse worked most of the time; few people were rude enough to interrupt someone's dinner.

"The point is..." interrupted Mrs Flanagan, Daisy could almost hear her sit up straighter in an attempt to put her point across, "...he ...we ...do not think it is appropriate to advertise for a dogging assistant, at all, let alone through a school."

"Fine, alright, thank you for letting me know. Goodbye."

Daisy was furious when she got off the phone, *how dare they, seriously, how was advertising for a dogwalker assistant such a big issue that the headteacher would ring her at home and the diocese were involved. God, there would be pitchforks at dawn. Whatever was the problem with this stupid place.* Daisy was furious. She swore under her breath as she dished up dinner and instructed the children to wash their hands and sit down nicely.

While she was washing up, Daisy rang Georgie for a rant. She could not believe that the school had made such a fuss about her leaflet. She had just about managed to eat dinner and pretend to be calm and smiley but Sally had asked her what her headteacher had wanted to talk to her about. Daisy had simply replied that she had wanted to discuss her dogwalking business; it was not quite a lie, she had.

Georgie was pleased to hear from her and was ready for more questions about the weekend. Daisy reassured her that all was well in terms of the packing but then went on to tell her about the conversation with the school. Georgie was always a good choice of friend to bitch with and she settled down ready to hear all the ins and outs of this rude headteacher's phonecall.

"So what did the flyer say?" asked Georgie.

"Just the same as last time really, with an added part on the bottom advertising for an assistant."

"Really, how ridiculous."

Daisy dried her hands and loaded up the computer, she wanted to see for sure what it was that had caused so much fuss. She read it out to Georgie. Strangely, Georgie burst out laughing and Daisy was concerned for her welfare as she coughed, spluttered, and howled with laughter down the phone. Daisy knew that she had a wicked sense of humour but she felt it was a tad insensitive bearing in mind she knew how upset and angry Daisy was about the matter.

Eventually the laughing and choking subsided and Georgie caught her breath.

"What?" asked Daisy, quite hurt by her friend's reaction.

"Oh sweety, do you not know?"

"Know what?" Daisy felt as though she might cry.

"Is your computer on?"

"Yes."

"Ok, youtube 'Fascinating Aida'." She spelt it out while Daisy typed. 'Right, now find the 'dogging song'."

As the video loaded and Daisy had checked on the location of the children, as advised by Georgie, she listened in horror. She had not even known that dogging meant that! She had simply thought it sounded like a more fun way to word it. Apparently according to Georgie and the lady singing, it was a much more fun job to be a dogging assistant.

Seeing the funny side of this now, Daisy was in stitches. Also she was mortified that she had handed these out, but more so she wondered how many applicants she would get. Some knowing what she actually meant and others assuming her dogwalking business was a cover for what she really did. Daisy put her head in her hands. Thankfully Georgie was cultured and had seen them live in Lincoln the other month. The singers, not the doggers. Daisy had given out over a hundred flyers and shared the picture of it on Facebook. *Oh God.* As Georgie's chuckles rung out down the phone, Daisy wondered if she should change the kids' school and deactivate her Facebook. She was never going to live this down. Ever.

The children came running out to see what all the noise was about. Daisy closed the laptop and hugged them both to reassure them. Daisy told them that she would be going in to speak to Mrs Flanagan tomorrow morning, but that they had nothing to worry about, they were not in trouble. She was still smirking and the children gave her the look of 'bless her', she was used to this.

Who had been more embarrassed by the explanation of the dogging advertisement was still unsure. Mrs Flanagan had apparently been no more informed about dogging than Daisy, however the cause for concern seemed to lean more towards Vicar Dean, who had known exactly what it was. Neither Daisy nor Mrs Flanagan had pushed this line of thought. They decided instead to quickly change the subject towards that of the children and how well they were both doing.

Georgie had still been thoroughly entertained by the entire subject and by the time Daisy and the children arrived Friday evening, Georgie could be heard randomly humming the 'dogging song' while pottering around in the kitchen. Obviously the children were unaware of the tune and Daisy could not help but feel thankful she hadn't known the words. It did, however, cheer her up after a long drive stuck behind caravans heading for Skegness and tractors heading home for their tea.

The children were so excited to finally arrive in Lincoln after all their research and were prepared to go straight to the castle on arrival. It was not that they didn't like Georgie; they seemed to like her very much. However they felt that if she hadn't been so keen on tea and cake that the castle trip could be underway already. Instead they were informed by Daisy that they would have to wait until tomorrow. The sulking subsided quickly once they saw the cake. It was a huge victoria sponge with cream and fresh strawberries laid delicately on and around it. Their eyes nearly popped out of their heads at the sight of it and it tasted even better than it looked.

Sally asked if her teddies could join them, as they loved tea parties. Georgie jumped at the idea of this and nipped upstairs to fetch them a proper tartan picnic blanket and a couple of friends. She laid the blanket out and introduced Sally to her teddies, they all made friends and both the children sat on the floor to join them. Georgie had a natural way with children and Daisy could not understand why it was that Georgie's daughter didn't tap into this more. It must be lovely for her to have children in the house again but heart-breaking at the same time.

After their tea party, Georgie showed them the rooms they would be staying in. She had gone to so much trouble to arrange everything for their visit; it was hard to determine who was most excited. She had not only cleared out all the junk, with Stephan's help, but she had put up fresh curtains, with tiny rose buds on them. She had purchased a couple of divan beds from a friend and she proudly showed off the pictures she had found in charity shops and the rug, which was beautiful. So as to make the children comfortable she had set up a bedside table each with their own lamp. The duvet covers were pink for Sally with princesses on and blue with dinosaurs on for Cory. It looked beautiful and both the children thanked her with hugs and went and sat on their beds, huge smiles on their faces. Daisy hugged Georgie tight.

"Thank you so much, you really didn't need to go through so much trouble."

"Oh, it was no trouble; I actually really enjoyed doing it. I needed an excuse to sort it out to be honest and you have given me one. We had great fun."

An image of Stephan hauling the furniture around, possibly topless, slipped into her mind, just as he appeared behind her, fully clothed.

"Hello trouble, how you doing?"

"I'm good thank you," they hugged, she felt his muscular arms flex as he squeezed her tight, her knees wobbled a little bit, "we were just admiring all yours and Georgie's hard work, it looks amazing."

"It certainly is a huge change," he laughed.

Chapter Twenty-Three- Lincoln Nights

Daisy set to tucking the children in for the night while Georgie and Stephan cleaned up after tea. Cory and Sally chatted away excitedly as they got in their pyjamas and unpacked their bags, popping everything neatly away in the bedside cabinets. Daisy could not have been more grateful to Georgie for letting them stay but also organising the room like this meant the children were too thrilled to be argumentative about the fact it was bedtime. She took them downstairs for teeth and toilets and they hugged Georgie goodnight and simply bidded 'night' to Stephan. After a quick story they snuggled down with kisses and cuddles, leaving Daisy to relax with friends for the evening.

"Did they go down alright?" enquired Georgie.

"Yep, not a cross word or a complaint. Thank you so much for letting us stay and they love the room."

Georgie batted away the gratitude with her hand, "The least I could do, they are wonderful children."

"They really are," chipped in Stephan.

"Ah thank you, I'm amazed at how well they have behaved. To be honest part of me was dreading bringing them in case they played up," she corrected herself, feeling guilty for seeming as though she was slagging off her own children, "Not that they normally do, it is just that this is the first time I have taken them away on my own."

"I knew what you meant," said Georgie, "It is a scary concept with children, they are so unpredictable. But they are a credit to you, you are a wonderful mother."

Daisy stayed silent and just smiled, it was nice for her to hear that she was doing a good job. She had felt so tired lately and as though she did not pay them as much attention as she should that the mother guilt had been building up. The weekend away was almost a thank you gesture to her children for them supporting her. Yet, as it was the children loved her new job as much as she did. They joined her on her afternoon walks and on the weekends they loved the fact that they got to play on the park while she ran the dogs on the field.

Thinking about it, the job had probably brought them closer as a family because she made the effort to get up and out. It gave her a reason to function in order to offer a punctual and effective service. All the dogs were very good at being walked by the children too, she would not have accepted any which were not good around children. So she took a deep breath, followed by a gulp of wine provided by Stephan as she had entered the room. It really did seem as though he was trying to wean her into alcoholism. She took another mouthful and simultaneously breathed out all her mother guilt. In fact maybe she could take on some mother pride in herself for doing a good job, as Georgie had stated.

It was so nice to spend the evening back in Georgie's cosy living room, the company was good, the conversation was entertaining and the wine was flowing gratefully through their veins, easing the tension out. *This was the life.* All of a sudden Georgie jumped up, Stephan and Daisy sat up straight ready to tackle a giant spider or fight off a moth.

"I have something for you," she aimed at Daisy. Both Daisy and Stephan relaxed their stances.

"Dare I ask?" Daisy could never be sure quite what Georgie had planned, *had she been on another shopping spree in Ann Summers? Was she about to pull out a giant Tom in front of Stephan?*

"Here," she handed her a DVD. Daisy turned the case over and burst out laughing.

Stephan leant over to see what it was and they all laughed now, obviously Stephan had been filled in on her mishap, in fact she had an idea that she might have told him via Facebook, it was all a blur. Her mind had set up an emotional block to protect her sanity.

"I remembered that I had bought the DVD after seeing them in Lincoln last year, they were so funny, I couldn't not."

Georgie asked Stephan to set up the DVD player, she admitted that she still didn't have a clue how it worked. He did, and then refilled all their glasses as they settle back to watch 'Fascinating Aida'. Daisy could not wait, just that one song, as mortifyingly embarrassed as she had been at the time, was hilarious. The three of them were crying with laughter the whole way through and they were holding their stomachs as the muscles were screaming in pain equally as much as they were screaming with laughter. Bearing in mind the strength of the wine which Stephan had provided they were all quite merry by the end of the DVD and the second bottle.

"Honestly, I have never laughed so much in my life!" exclaimed Georgie.

"Me either," agreed Daisy as she rubbed her tummy to try to sooth it.

"Or me, I'm gutted I didn't get to see them when they were here," Stephan added.

"They are fabulous indeed," slurred Georgie.

It really had been a wonderful evening and Daisy headed off to bed content and sleepy from all the wine. Her cheeks and stomach ached from all the laughing and she was still smiling to herself as she got changed for bed. She slipped back down the stairs after checking on the children, who were snug as bugs. After she had cleaned her teeth she padded through the kitchen back up to the bedroom. Just as she reached the bottom of the stairs Stephan rounded the corner from the lounge carrying the empty bottles and glasses. The expert he was he hardly flinched, whereas Daisy screamed, then muffled it, hand over her mouth, so as not to wake the children. Georgie flew out of the room but burst out laughing again when she realised it was nothing to worry about.

Georgie giggled her way up to bed past the two of them. Stephan was holding her gaze and she smiled awkwardly, unsure of her next move, or if she even wanted to move. She was aware that they had both consumed a lot of alcohol but she was not swaying too much, although she believed the wall she was leaning on was assisting.

"I've had a lovely evening," he declared.

"Yes, me too," she agreed.

"I still laugh every time I think of you sending out your advertisement for a dogging assistant," they both laughed, "I'm surprised you didn't get a better response." He winked at her and her knees lost their support. As much as she would have loved to have attributed it to the wine she knew it was the intensity of his gaze and the effect his closeness was having on her.

Daisy cleared her throat. "I best get to bed," she almost whispered.

"Yea, me too, I'm gonna sofa it tonight, I don't think it is sensible to drive."

"Indeed."

Neither one of them had moved, even after their statements. Stephan really did have the most penetrating eyes. It was as though he could see straight into her soul; read her mind and know her every desire. They seemed to have been drawn closer to each other and she placed her hand on his shoulder for support. He was still holding the items but moved them to his side as he joined her in the space that had been between them. She felt her breath mingle with hers and was thankful that she had cleaned her teeth moments before. His breath smelt of pure testosterone and her body reacted accordingly.

"Mum," shouted Cory's voice from the top of the stairs.

Daisy turned as swiftly as the child had arrived, instantly in mothermode. She made her way up the stairs and led her son down towards the bathroom. Stephan simply continued his task of cleaning up the disarray of their evening's antics. The moment had been broken so abruptly that she questioned whether it had even happened at all. *Was he actually planning to kiss her? Was he going to try to kiss her again?* Her knees felt weak as she stood outside the bathroom door, she leant on the wall for support once more. The presence of Stephan behind her almost warming her aura. She turned to acknowledge him being there but as she did she saw only the back of him retreating into the living room to take up residence on the sofa. Her heart sunk slightly, she wanted nothing more than to curl up on the sofa with him, snuggle close and fall asleep in his arms. But the abrupt appearance of Cory broke her out of her fantasy.

As she laid in bed minutes later her son wrapped in her arms, she had not argued when he had protested about returning to his bed. In fact, she welcomed the comfort which came from his soft breathing next to her. Her mind was still fuzzy from the wine but as she drifted into a drunken sleep she questioned her thoughts about Stephan. *Had he actually been making an advance on her or was it more a case of the wine in both of them which had lead to them both 'thinking' that was what they had wanted. They were good friends, there was no denying that, however even though they had conversed regularly on Facebook, there had never been anything between them than mere friendship. Well there had been the odd light flirting but in general just friendly bantering rather than the consideration of anything more than that. Yes, he was gorgeous, but he was far too young and handsome for her; a divorced mother of two. God, that sounded bad phrased like that.* Cory shifted in his sleep. She hugged him and moved further over to give him more space. Sleep caught up with her and the image of Stephan in her mind sent her off to the world of dreams.

At five o'clock in the morning, she was jolted out of her dreamstate and back into reality. She was burning hot and Cory had luckily not been disturbed. She crept out from under the duvet, holding down the closest bit to Cory so the draft of her movement did not disturb him. Over the years she had become an expert ninja in such manoeuvres. Thank God she had done yoga a few times, it had kept her flexible. The stairs creaked underfoot, she had forgotten just how noisy they were. The eyes of the pictures seemed to follow her as she tried to stealthily get to the bottom, she needed a cup of coffee, more importantly she needed a wee.

She was startled as she entered the kitchen, Stephan was stood by the sink, sipping a hot cup of tea.

"I made you a coffee, I figured you'd need it." He gestured towards the side where the kettle stood.

"Oh, thank you," was all she could manage to muster. She really hadn't expected to find anyone up and about at this unholy hour.

From the silence upstairs it seemed as though the children and Georgie had not been disturbed by her waking. She reached for her drink, all thoughts of needing the toilet dissipated. Almost without him moving he was next to her, his breath sending shivers through her body. *He was so close, possibly too close, no not close enough.* She needed him closer. She put down her drink, not taking her eyes of him, his drink had gone too. She grabbed for him, pulling him closer, she needed him, right here, right now. She had never felt such a surge of passion for anyone, not even Tristan.

They ended up wrapped in each other's arms, the intensity overwhelming them both, pushing them closer and closer, until they could hardly work out whose limbs were whose. Whose breath was whose. With anyone else it would have scared her, made her self-conscious but right here, right now, it was exactly the right thing to be doing. Before she realised what was happening they were fully entwined. His body was so toned, so tight, so attractive. She wasn't even thinking about hers, she was fully in the heat of the moment.

They ended up on the sofa, snuggled as she had previously imagined. This was perfect, this was where she belonged, as life should be. She was euphoric.

Daisy awoke alone, in the bed in Georgie's spare room, the distant sound of chatting and laughter rang out from downstairs. It took her a moment to realise where she was. She physically and mentally checked in with herself. She dragged herself out of bed and downstairs to check on the children. She well and truly had another hangover, *had she not promised herself she wouldn't drink so much again? Maybe Stephan's ploy to turn her into an alcoholic was paying off.* She would have figured that she would have got used to the feeling given her recent conduct.

As much as she had now realised that her interaction with Stephan was simply a dream, it did not however stop her blushing when she meet him in the kitchen.

"Er, morning," she stuttered as she shuffled past him to the bathroom.

Daisy was becoming adverse to downstairs toilets- it left a person with very little privacy, or more to the point, time in which to pretty oneself before having to face others. The children were outside the door as she exited the bathroom and hugged her tight, as though they had not seen her for a year. They chatted loudly and told her all about their morning so far and the names of Georgie's teddies and Stephan's favourite teddy when he was a lad. Daisy listened as best she could and simultaneously edged forwards towards the kettle and headache tablets. Once the children had finished their update they ran back off to the living room, leaving her and Stephan alone.

Up until now she had not felt overly uncomfortable in his company, in fact, before the dream they had been very comfortable in each other's presence. As she poured out the hot water the memory of their 'almost embrace' last night, popped back up in her head. She just stopped herself from spilling it all over her hand. She really was a wreck this morning.

"You ok?" he enquired from behind her.

"Yes, yes I'm fine, just a bit of a headache," she tried to look comfortable but struggled as he was so close once more. Instead she came off as acting abrasive towards him.

"Oh, sorry," he scuttled off to join the others.

She mentally kicked herself for being so rude. He wasn't to know they had made passionate love right here in this exact spot, but only in her dream. But dreams as vivid as that one, stayed with her, this one she wanted to file as a memory. Freud would have had a field day with her mind, it was textbook lusting.

Chapter Twenty-Four- Steep Hill

Once everyone was up and about they set off to explore Lincoln. Stephan had gone to work an hour or so ago. It was only as the front door had closed behind him that Daisy finally breathed. Why she had felt so tense when nothing had actually happened she had no idea. She considered that it could be because she now wished something had transpired. In fact, she was actually feeling quite down about the lack of activity between them. He oozed sex-appeal and the pheromones floating around made her feel like a wonton woman. She had never considered herself an attractive woman in the sense of others lusting after her, until recently. It had become a regular occurrence to be told that she was 'looking well' and she found herself spending more time in front of the mirror than she had before. She had even started buying matching sets of underwear, just in case.

The problem was, however, that between the reappearance of Tristan and Stephan becoming close friends, Daisy was confused. It was not her intention to mislead either of them but somehow she found herself holding them both close while still at arm's length. She knew, of course, that her mixed signals were not helping anyone. She justified it with the fact that it had been a long time since she had dated or spent much time with single men. The most disconcerting fact of all was that she wasn't entirely sure they were even interested in her as anything more than a friend. Hopefully she would get a chance to talk things though with Georgie, she was always good at putting things into perspective. She might also be able to shine some light on the Stephan situation.

The children were so excited. They had been in the kitchen for ages with Georgie, preparing a picnic. Georgie was so good with them, a true natural, they adored her. Daisy tried to get herself dressed and ready as quickly as possible, no matter how many times Georgie told her to relax, she felt bad putting all the responsibly on her, that was not the reason she had visited.

The children listed off all the items in the picnic to Daisy as she entered the kitchen.

"Wow, you really have prepared a feast for us."

"There is a big flask of strong coffee too," Georgie smirked.

"Fab." All else aside, coffee was a necessity today.

Her headache was fading but she still felt a bit dozy. The fresh air should help. She was very much looking forward to their day out together, she hadn't explored castles since she was a kid. The cathedral looked stunning enough from the outside so she could only imagine how impressive the interior would be. They all slipped on their shoes and jackets and set off.

Although she had known there would be hills she had not quite prepared herself for Steep Hill. In fact, other than mountaineering, nothing much could have equipped her. The children ran on ahead as Daisy and Georgie huffed and puffed their way upwards. Daisy used the excuse of stopping intermittently to look into all the quaint little shops which ordained either side. Each time they paused Daisy took deep breaths and wiped her brow. Thank God she had been doing so much walking lately or else they would have had to call the paramedics to revive her. *So much for being fit and healthy!*

Daisy gasped at the sight laid out before her. The Steep Hill now got truly steep, it was practically vertical. There were railings in place along the edge of the path and the cobbles, this was not a good sign. The path was practically vertical and Daisy and Georgie worked together to help each other up the hill. The children on the other hand raced each other, laughing and taking the mickey out of their mother and her friend. Then jogging past them all came a young woman pushing a buggy, dressed in sports gear, this was obviously her daily workout!

Just at the point where she thought she might die from the exertion the roadway flattened out. *Phew.* Somehow the children were still running and laughing and thoroughly enjoying their hillwalking experience. Georgie pointed out the 'Bookstop Café' in the basement of an old building. Georgie explained that the owner had started up earlier in the year. An author himself he had seen a niche in the market and stocked self-published authors. Also there were shelves of second hand books, and a children's section, she informed the children, who had run back to join them.

"Cool, can we go in there?" asked Sally animatedly, eyes wide with intrigue.

"Not just yet, we could go in on the way back down."

"I hear," whispered Georgie conspiratorially, "that he has the most delicious cakes and milkshakes." The children's eyes grew wider. "After we have seen the castle and cathedral we will pop in and say hello. I think he writes children's books himself."

"Could we buy some books Mum?"

"Maybe. We could do with some new books to read, couldn't we?"

That satisfied their questioning for now and they got ready to venture on again. Having caught their breath they pushed on. Daisy observed that the people coming down the hill had a look of pity and relief. Struggling tourists were obviously a common sight on Steep Hill and she could only imagine the amusement of the shop owners who people watched. It was a mixture of age ranges and footwear choices that kept Daisy's mind off the burning feeling in her lungs and the screams of her calf muscles.

Just outside a cute little teashop was a lady wearing the most fabulous pair of purple boots. Under normal circumstances she would have looked at her with pure envy. She watched her edge sideways, clinging onto the walls as she carefully placed onfoot then the other on the vertical pavement. Wobbling on the three inch heels, which would have earned her money in another profession. The boots were beautiful in all fairness, when Daisy braved looking up from her footings, the lady was beautiful. But the wobbling unsteadiness of her decent was ungainly. She lowered her gaze again, wiped her brow and dug in her heels with renewed vigour. If nothing else she was almost at the top and she was wearing sensible, comfy shoes that in no way hindered this difficult enough of climbs; and her walk down would not be anywhere near as difficult. She smiled kindly at the lady as she sped up past her.

Georgie was staring at the cakes in the window of the teashop and Daisy joined her to gaze longingly at them. Then they pointed out the lamps which were made up of beautiful crockery with lampshades on top. She scooted the children off quickly as they came running back to join them, the last thing she needed was them trying to design similar artwork at home. As much as she didn't own anything as close to posh as these, she did not have any to spare for such things. The cakes looked far too delicious to pass by but because their willpower was so strong and they were so close to the old district they ploughed on and they had vowed to pop in to the Bookstop Cafè on their way back down.

As the castle came into view the children once more ran on ahead, Daisy and Georgie walked faster to keep up with them, thankful it was flat ground up here. Daisy felt the childish bubble of excitement as they strode under the archway leading to the gift shop. The toy swords, shields and replicas appealed to her childish side, she wanted to kit both the children out in tiny knight outfits and run around the castle chasing each other. She was so pleased to have finally made it up to the castle (more like survived, the climb up the hill and here) it was magical.

Daisy was not a fan of heights but the kids were begging to walk along the top of the castle wall. Taking a deep breath, Daisy led the way up the stone steps, Cory followed, then Sally, and Georgie who appeared to be as equally enthralled by the whole experience. They all pretended to fire bows and arrows from the battlements. Daisy's knees were slightly jellified but the wind on their faces, the laughter in her ears and the entire event meant that she pushed past the fear. It was not to say it disappeared, she wished, but she just focused on the moment, channelling her fear. Cory was not as convinced by the whole pretence and held her hand tight. Daisy foresaw a kind hearted and considerate man and felt that she was bringing her children up well.

The moment was superseded when they moved across to the prison section and the children decided that locking Mummy up would be hilarious. Georgie told them they could not just lock her up they would have to take her to court first to find a reason to. Sally figured that the chapel would make a perfect court room. The whole thing played out well until Georgie opened a door to find a mannequin posing as a prisoner. Her screaming amused the children and Daisy for the rest of the visit. As a family wandered into the chapel and looked bemused by their upbeat behaviour but on the other hand it cheered them up.

They sat in the grounds under the beady eyes of the statue and while the adults set up the picnic rug and food, the children joined forces with other children. They formed two armies, one of boys, one of girls. The adults sitting around seemed unnerved by this. It was great to see them all enjoying themselves but as they had all now visited the prison cells, they knew to watch their backs. Bribery of delicious sandwiches and sweet treats might keep them out of the cells long enough to drink the flask of coffee.

They had a wonderful time relaxing in the sunshine, surrounded by history and culture and excitable children. All the children nipped back to their parents intermittently, took huge bites of food, gulped drinks and ran off to carry on their games. Daisy revelled in the fact that it had cost them less than £20 to get in and yet the day had been a success in every way. Georgie and Daisy sunned themselves and put the world to rights while the laughter echoed around them. Many days had been spent at more commercial places, supposedly aimed at amusing the whole family, full of magic and fun. More often than not, they had been nightmare days that instead of being full of such advertised joy was in reality full of shouting and whingeing and tears; usually Daisy's. This in contrast was perfect. All the adults looked equally relaxed and the youngsters were thoroughly enjoying themselves and interacting with others rather than technology or thrill-seeking rides. Daisy and Georgie simultaneously sighed contently, momentarily closing their eyes.

"Got you!" screamed the five little monsters who had seen a moment of weakness.

"Ahhhh," screamed the shocked pair, both of whom had now jumped to their feet and were being chased. Not for a second did the thought cross their minds of who might steal their belongings as they ran around. It was not even a consideration that people around them might judge them as their wobbly bits wobbled. They were truly in the moment and the children were all the happier for seeing them joining in carelessly.

Just as Daisy was hiding behind a tree, Georgie being the prime target, arms encased her tightly, she froze. These were not the arms of a child.

"Caught you."

She twisted in the manly arms and met the eyes of Stephan, amusement shone out and she sniggered. He held her and yelled to the children that he had captured the prisoner. They ran over to take her to her doom. Daisy threw him the death stare and he simply winked back. Whether it was the fatigue of her muscles from the hill-climbing and the running or pure energy propelled in her direction. Either way he once again melted her supposedly strong façade.

Chapter Twenty-Five- The Decent

By the time the adventures of the castle were over everyone was in high spirits but fully aware of the walk home ahead of them. The promise of cake had not been forgotten; mainly by Georgie. They had decided to leave the cathedral visit for another day and the children begged to return to the castle another day and demanded that Stephan join them, according to them he had been the most fun. Part of Daisy was pleased, the other more selfish Mum side of her wondered how come she was not deemed the most fun, it could not be denied that she had played along just as much. Stephan promised he would try to come again with them and informed them that it was the most fun he had had in ages. Apparently, neither he nor Georgie had ever taken the time to visit the castle before. Daisy guessed it was true of most people's home towns or cities, you never took the time to do the tourist bit. She vowed to investigate more of their home town.

The cake and coffee in the Bookstop Cafè was as delicious as she had anticipated. The children enjoyed a hot chocolate which came served in a child-size cup and saucer, with marshmallows and a spoon to scoop them out. It had been a long time since she had seen her offspring looking so elated, she sat back and just observed their happy, slightly flushed faces. As she redirected her gaze her eyes met Stephan's, he had been watching the way she lovingly looked at her children, pure devotion emulating from her motherly regard. She blushed slightly and took another fork full of cake; hoping that he would redirect his attention.

Georgie was showing the children around, they had chosen a handful of books each, and Georgie waved away Daisy's offer to pay for them.

"My treat," she confirmed.

Georgie and the children stood chatting to Joff the owner, he was telling the children all about the history of the building and listened as they regaled the antics of their afternoon. They were enthralled by it all and Daisy realised that it was just her and Stephan left at the table when he moved to the seat next to her.

"Isn't this a lovely little place?"

"Yes, it really is, I would spend all my time here if I lived closer. I could just see myself curled up on the sofa with a constant supply of coffee, cake and good books."

"I agree. I would love nothing more than to join you."

The silence fell between them, with the image of the two of them cuddled up on the sofa, contently reading and relaxing. That picture encapsulated exactly what Daisy wished for in life; quite contentment with a companion. She felt she was too old now to expect passion and steamy sex on sofas. In fact, possibly that was where her marriage to Joel had worked, they were content with each other. She yearned for that again with someone. A person who would gently place a blanket over her while she laid on the sofa reading. Someone who would make her coffee, knowing that she needed the energy to get through the bedtime routine with the children. Someone who would sit next to her as she read to the children at night and enjoy the story just as much as they did. In a nutshell, someone she could be comfortable around; be herself.

"Mum," she woke from her daydream to see Cory and Sally standing, hands behind their backs, big beaming smiles across their cute little faces. "We got you something, close your eyes." The giggling continued and they placed something into her outstretched hands. It was a book, obviously, but not just any book, it was the first in the 'Inkheart' trilogy. She had expressed ages ago that it was a film she had enjoyed and would love to read the books as they were meant to be even better. She hugged them tight, and then stood to hug Georgie. They were pleased she liked it and they then talked her through their books.

Stephan read part of one of Sally's books to her. A lump appeared in her throat and she scrapped her hair back behind her ear and finished her coffee; now was not the time to get over whelmed with emotion. A man paying attention to her children was not a sign of anything other than the fact that he liked them as a family. In no way; either in her imagination or anywhere else was it a sign he wanted to play happy families with them. She reminded herself that although he was a good friend, that was in fact all he was and he was mainly here just to spend time with his aunt. They were just a consolation price.

She straightened up and Cory read a couple of pages of his book out to her. Some of Cory's crumbs dropped in between the pages and she tried to pretend that she didn't feel Stephan staring at her again. However, she enjoyed the concept that her simple motherly duties caught his eye. Georgie was still chatting to Joff about his books and cake recipes. Daisy admired her ease with people, the way she just seemed to know what to say and to whom. Unfortunately, Daisy did not have this attribute; she was always awkward and nervous around people, the ultimate, 'put her foot into it' type. So as to avoid these situations she simply stayed quiet most of the time unless someone made conversation with her. Even so, this never completely saved her.

The descent was much easier than the climb, apart from the overwhelming feeling of falling. Sally and Cory raced off ahead but with slightly less energy. The adults meandered along behind, carefully watching their footing. The fear of falling was almost comparable to the concern of death on the way up but she found herself looking at the people heading up the hill with pity. She wanted to advise them to turn around or offer them water to assist their climb but she refrained. As difficult as the climb had been it had been worth it, they had thoroughly enjoyed themselves.

Stephan and Georgie had linked arms and were in fits of laughter, Georgie intermittently whooped as she lost her footing and Stephan nearly slid with her a couple of times. Daisy smiled at them, they were such a fab family. If the rest of them were anything like these two she could only imagine that a family party would be a hoot. Images flashed through her mind while she watched them, her cheeks were aching from the smiling and laughing she had done this weekend.

She felt completely relaxed and happy, a feeling that had gradually replaced the fearful, agitated ones which had haunted her after her marriage had broken down. Yet with good friends around her, her children being happy and her business doing well they had all contributed to her successful journey to being a fulfilled individual. Thus, she felt she was a better mother, friend and person in general. Whilst she had initially stumbled around in the world of the singletons with an overwhelming feeling of failure that was all-consuming. Caching her reflection now in the window of a cute little gift shop, she saw a genuinely confident lady looking back at her. It was almost inconceivable that this transformation had happened so quickly and without her conscious realisation. She gave her reflection an apprehensive smile and turned her attention back to the matter in hand.

From the cackles ahead Daisy could only assume that Georgie was still struggling but on turning the corner she was faced with the actuality. Georgie was sat on the floor in the most unladylike fashion, Stephan was laughing too hard to help her up and the children had a hand each side of her and were attempting to haul her up. People were pausing to either just gawk, while others offered assistance. Daisy joined them in their endeavour but Georgie was laughing far too hard to even be lifted from the ground.

Finally, after much fuss, Georgie was upright once more. The children were still giggling and they decided that instead of attempting to take her down the rest of the hill they veered to the left and made their way through the Arboretum. Georgie was animatedly telling them all how she had slipped over and found it highly amusing that it had been on the one flat part. The children had agreed that Georgie could not be trusted to walk alone and that Stephan was not capable of looking after her properly. So Sally took one hand and Cory the other and they gaily walked along chatting and laughing.

Daisy became aware as she watched them of the fact that her and Stephan were left to walk together. Before the events and the dream of this weekend she would have been quite comfortable to wander along with him. But the dynamics had changed; he seemed to view her as more than just a friend and she was also starting to think along those lines. As nice an image as it was Daisy felt a pang similar to the one she felt with Tristan, in that 'friends' was a nice idea. Relationships on the other hand were complicated and full of moments like this where no one knows quite what to say or do. Part of her wanted to just grab his hand and skip along the road. She wondered how he would react if she was to just seize his hand and skip. *Would he join in or would he be appalled and never so much as send her a Facebook game request again?* So the sensible Daisy won out, she decided to just walk along like the grown-up she had seemingly become.

"It has been a really nice day, hasn't it?"

"Yes it really has," she agreed.

"You have a wonderful family Daisy, you should be very proud of yourself." He was looking at her intently.

Daisy was unaccustomed to compliments but did not want to appear rude so simply thanked him.

"Georgie is loving having the kids around," he continued. "it is such a shame that she doesn't see Casey and Grace more often."

"Yes, I agree."

The small-talk did the job and the awkwardness subsided. It was replaced with Stephan telling her stories about Georgie's daughter when she was younger and how she hadn't changed much. He expressed confusion about why it was she hated Georgie so much, he couldn't remember anything drastic enough for Casey to not want to have much to do with her Mum.

"See, I can't imagine not having contact with my Mum, but I'm really lucky, she is my rock," Daisy said.

"I guess, that's it, everyone's childhoods and relationships with their parents are very different, even in the same family."

Daisy wondered how her children would view her when they were adults, a shiver of concern rushed over her. *What if they hated her? What if they blamed her for the breakup? What if they moved as far away as they could in order to keep out of her way?* She hoped with all her heart that she would have a relationship with them like she had with her own Mum. It would mortify her to think that she had messed things up so bad that they wanted nothing to do with her. Watching them walking along with Georgie giggling and chatting she didn't think that the recent events had had too much of an impact so far. She decided to stop worrying, she would do her best and keep her fingers crossed that it all worked out ok. If, however, it didn't she would deal with it when it came. *No point worrying just yet.*

Chapter Twenty-Six- Posh Tea Party

Daisy sat dozing on the sofa at Georgie's. The children and Georgie were baking and Stephan had popped home to go sort something out. She laid there wondering how everyone except her seemed to be full of energy. It crossed her mind that if they lived in Lincoln how much fitter and healthier she would be. Walking the dogs would be a hike and a half, but Lord her figure would be stunning. As she drifted in and out of consciousness she imaged herself walking up the hill, the dogs dragging her up like huskies, her panting and crying in pain. Yet the dogs would be happy as Larry. She would have to ask Joff if he could have cold drinks and flannels at the ready. She would whizz past, the dogs not wanting to stop and she would grab the refreshments like a marathon runner. She smiled to herself and fell into a deep sleep, the exhaustion of her thoughts making her tired.

She awoke, seemingly moments later, to the children setting up the cake stand with fresh cakes and Georgie had helped them set up the table with a tablecloth, napkins, cups and saucers and little plates for the cakes. It looked beautiful and the pride on her children's faces was a wonderful sight. Sally had sat Georgie's favourite teddy on one chair and the other side of the table sat her favourite one and Cory had his teddy sat on his lap, napkin on his lap ready to test the cakes. Daisy voiced her admiration of their work.

"It is a proper grown up tea party, like posh people have," Cory informed her.

"Because we have been to a castle and we were so well behaved," added Sally.

Daisy kissed them both on the forehead and kissed Georgie on the cheek.

"Thank you, sorry I fell asleep," apologised Daisy to Georgie.

"Don't be silly, you deserve to relax, I love having something to do and people to do it with," she smiled, but her eyes showed a pang of sadness.

Daisy wondered whether there was anything she could do to try to ease the strained situation with Georgie's daughter. She knew it was not her place, she really had no idea what the reasons were; and there were always reasons. Although, being a friend to Daisy and spending time with her with or without the children would hopefully help her. Her daughter might come round eventually. Daisy's job was nothing more taxing than being a good friend and a source of support.

The seven of them sat round the elegantly laid table and they talked in posh voices, as apparently they had to, to be able to have a tea party. Daisy thoroughly enjoyed it, the children were glowing with excitement and Georgie was teaching them how to pat the corners of their mouths with their napkins. Cory's teddy was very skilled at this and Georgie swore that he had previously attended such events. Cory and Sally twittered as they helped the teddies to drink their tea. They told Daisy about the tea set and the fact it was really old and that it was Georgie's parents.

"When she was little she was not allowed to use it. That is why she loves using it now. Isn't she kind to let us?" Sally directed at Daisy.

"Very much so," concurred Daisy, "you are very honoured."

"Are we?" Cory looked upset.

Georgie reassured him, "That is a good thing, it means you are lucky."

"Oh," brightened up Cory.

Daisy stroked his arm to comfort him.

Just as they were finishing up, having tasted the delicious victoria sponge and the scones, the doorbell rang. The children ran after Georgie to see who it was, they really had settled in well considering it was their first visit here. There was a cheer and they re-entered the room with Stephan, each of them holding a hand. Georgie followed behind with another good-looking young man.

"Daisy this is Tom. Tom this is my good friend Daisy." Georgie had a troublesome glint in her eye and as Daisy stood to shake hands with him, she stifled a giggle.

"Nice to meet you Tom."

"Likewise," he seemed not to notice the looks passing between the two ladies. It was not until Daisy joined Georgie in the kitchen, where she was making a fresh pot of tea, that they allowed themselves a proper laugh. By the time they had recovered from their laughing fit the children had laid the teddies to one side and sat Tom and Stephan down. They busied themselves with gathering clean crockery for them and refilling the sugar cubes. Daisy beamed with pride. Tom and Stephan both played along with the posh voices. The children and Stephan told Tom all about their day out at a real castle. In return, he told them a childhood memory of visiting a castle where they had a re-enactment, which he explained meant that everyone dressed up as knights or maidens. Sally and Cory sipped their tea and listened intently. As he rounded off the story they turned to Daisy and asked if they could go to one.

"Yes, I'm sure we could, they do things like that at Castle Rising, we will find out about it."

"Yay!" they started to go in to the usual celebratory wriggle but remembered the special tea set and stopped themselves. Daisy observed this with wonder, maybe she should go charity shopping for posh looking crockery and they might behave better at the table at home. It was great to see that they were respectful in other people's houses. It was not that they were overly naughty at home but this behaviour was that of angelic children, the kind everyone else seemed to have. She sat up straighter with mother pride and gave them both a 'well done' smile. They beamed with pride.

Even after having a quick snooze earlier in the day, Daisy was yawning more than the children as she scooped them up to bed. She wiped the tears from her eyes as she read to them. The children were concerned that she was finding the story sad but she explained that it was because she was yawning and she knew the story had a happy ending. She kissed them both goodnight and told them how pleased she was that they had enjoyed their day and congratulated them on their fabulous behaviour.

Georgie was curled up in the armchair, cradling a cup of hot chocolate when Daisy entered the room.

"They ok?"

"Yea they went down no problem."

Georgie saw her watery eyes, "Are you ok?"

"Yea, just tired, the kids thought I'd been crying because I couldn't stop yawning and my eyes were watering. Bless 'em."

"Ah they are fabulous children, I'm so glad you brought them with you. I have thoroughly enjoyed today." Georgie pointed to the coffee table, "Yours is there sweety."

"Oh, thank you, you do know I'll be asleep in minutes at this rate," Daisy jested.

"No problem if you are, it has been a hectic few weeks for you. So how is the dog walking going?"

"Really well, I'm quite surprised it has had such a good response, hence the need for a dogging assistant!" She grinned at Georgie.

"Anyone apply yet?" She chuckled.

"Not as yet, thankfully." She sipped her hot chocolate and tried not to spill it as they laughed at her misdemeanour.

"So what have you done with the boys?" enquired Daisy.

"Oh, they headed back out, I think we bore them, too old." She was joking but Daisy wondered how she had suddenly become categorised as 'old' when Georgie was at least ten or so years older than her. Georgie obviously picked up on her thoughts, probably because of the gutted look on her face.

"Not you dear, I meant me."

Daisy was relieved but tried to hide it better than before. "Hardly," was the best she could offer in way of reassurance. She guessed that in all fairness a young good-looking couple of men did not want to spend their Saturday night in with cups of hot chocolate and two gossiping women. Part of her wished they had stayed but she also understood that in reality the lads would have been quite bored here. She had a pang of longing, wishing she could have joined them but then reminded herself that she was a responsible woman. Yet, she had a horrible feeling that Stephan might roll up tomorrow morning with tales of their amazing night out and the women he had pulled, a thought struck her; *what if he turned up with a woman?* Her stomach somersaulted at the thought.

"Is it too hot?" asked Georgie.

"What? Erm, no, no not at all, sorry."

"Honey you can head off to bed, I won't be far behind, I'm exhausted myself. I'm not sure though whether my tired legs can get me to the top of the stairs. I bet they'll be seized up tomorrow."

"God, yea, mine too." Daisy pushed the vision of Stephan snogging some young blonde to the back of her mind. *He was just a friend. A stunningly handsome friend but nevertheless only a friend.*

"By the way, how funny was that earlier when Tom turned up?" Georgie blurted.

"Oh, that was so funny, it took all my willpower not to laugh right at him. Can you imagine if he ever found out about your little friend?"

"Less of the little," Georgie said straight-faced.

Daisy nearly spat her hot chocolate right across the room. She held up her hand to stop Georgie from proceeding along this line of conversation. She quickly placed her cup on the table.

"Georgie you are terrible!"

"Speaking of terrible I was thinking. Should we book an Ann Summers party? It would be great fun. I could ask down at the coffee morning if anyone would be interested. You'd be surprised what a randy bunch they are down there."

While Daisy tried to process this suggestion Georgie started reeling off names of possible candidates and their marital status. Most of them were either divorced or widowed. "Perfect, they could all use a good Tom in their lives."

It was the serious expression on Georgie's face as she said this that sent Daisy over the edge. She could not breathe she was laughing so much, and although Georgie was too, she didn't seem to realise why this was so funny. She was being practical; not all husbands would want their wives to be buying 'toys'. When she voiced this, Daisy laughed even harder. This was not the kind of conversation she had expected when she had first meet Georgie back in London, quite the opposite in fact.

After much more laughing and discussion about who may or may not attend, and whose pension would not cover the cost of a 'Tom', they decided Georgie would ask around before booking it. Obviously, they would have to book it on a weekend Daisy was childfree, the long-term psychological damage on witnessing that would be immense. Daisy was a tad concerned about her own psychological stability but thought that she would at least be able to process the information properly, her children, on the other hand, would not.

Just as they were closing up the house for the night there was a tap on the door. Both women looked at each other, then at the clock. It was nearly midnight and neither one of them moved to open it, they instead stood frozen to the spot, holding their breath. There was another knock on the door, slightly louder this time. Georgie moved to the living room window to see who it could be and Daisy was right behind her. She knew that Georgie rarely got visitors, let alone this late at night. Georgie turned and shrugged and pulled a face to show she had no idea. After one more knock, the person was obviously keen to get their attention, they went to the door and unlocked it, slowly edging the door open until they could see who it was. Daisy had her mobile in her hand ready to call the police if they needed to.

"I'm sorry I didn't mean to scare you but is Daisy there?"

Daisy stepped forward, and Georgie looked at her with confusion.

"Joel, what are you doing here?"

"Sorry," he slurred.

He was about to start telling them why when Georgie interrupted him. "Come in, you'll wake the whole neighbourhood."

They guided him in, he reeked of alcohol. Georgie put the kettle on; he needed coffee and by the looks of things the two of them would need one to keep them awake through whatever drama had arrived on the doorstep. Daisy sat Joel down in the living room.

"So what's up?"

"Well, I took your advice and came up here to experience the gay scene you had recommended up in

Lincoln." He looked at her with woeful eyes. "You were right it is fun but then I overheard some people talking about a day out they had had with their kids and I got all upset. I realised I missed the children and no amount of male attention, 'cos I got a lot tonight…" Daisy nodded, always the belle of the ball her Joel, "…would replace the loss of our family, of not seeing the kids enough. I missed you all and I remembered you had said you were up here this weekend so I had to come and see you. Thank God you gave me the address. Are the kids still up?"

"Joel, it is midnight and no they are fast asleep. I'm sorry you are finding it hard without us but we agreed that you couldn't, we couldn't…" she corrected herself, "…keep living a lie. The children are coping really well with the situation and I thought you were too. The best of both worlds."

"I thought so too." He started to cry and Daisy hugged him. He leaned into her and wrapped his strong arms around her. She wondered how other women coped with this. *Did other men do this to their exes? Was this just the drink talking or was he wanting to come to some different arrangement?* She hoped beyond anything that he was not about to suggest a reconciliation of the family, one which involved him spending some weekends out with his friends and she just got to play the happy wife and pretend the gay thing did not exist. *How would that even work?* She asked herself. *Not well she decided.* His sobs subsided and Georgie brought him his coffee and a box of tissues.

"Thank you," he said as he tried to compose himself. Daisy held the coffee while he blew his nose. "Sorry, I'm such a twat."

"You're fine." *What else could she say? Yes you are. Now stop this ridiculous gay stage and let's put our family back together as it should be before you decided to be a twat.* She was not convinced that this line of attack would solve anything so she kept quiet while he drunk his coffee.

She nipped into the kitchen where Georgie was taking as long as possible to tidy up and make their coffees.

"I'm sorry, Georgie."

"It's fine honey, don't fret. He obviously just needed to have a good old cry about it and for some reason you are the safest person to open up to. I'm going to head up to bed. If he wants to stay he's more than welcome. I'll leave it up to you."

"Thank you, you are too kind." Daisy gave her a hug and she passed her the coffee.

Chapter Twenty-Seven- Family Time

Sally and Cory were extremely excited to see Joel in the morning. It did, however, confuse them slightly that he was in Daisy's bed instead of her. The questions were relentless and it seemed that in his hungover state Joel did not appreciate it. Daisy found it quite amusing to watch, because for once it was not her suffering. She smirked to herself as she made her way downstairs to find them both a strong coffee. Her for shock, his to sober him up enough to drive home later.

Georgie said nothing other than 'yes please' for the proffered coffee. Daisy admired her approach to the bizarre situation that had arrived on her doorstep in the middle of the night. Daisy, of course, apologised for the awkwardness and thanked her for her understanding. Daisy was nonplussed by his sudden appearance and confession. Georgie was just happy to have someone else to make the coffee.

The children allowed Joel five minutes reprieve to go to the toilet before they were jumping all over him again. Moments later the doorbell rang. Georgie, who was leaning against the sink, carried her toast and plate to the door with her. Stephan came in and the children swapped their attention to him. Momentarily Joel looked relieved but then he seemed curious. Daisy introduced them and watched closely as Joel eyed Stephan. He did not seem too pleased to see his children happy around another male. In fact, he looked intrigued by the situation and even in his fragile state had puffed out to exude his masculinity. Stephan did not immediately register his existence, although Daisy was unsure as to how he could not have noticed he was there, the kitchen was not that big.

The children finally settled down for breakfast and at this point Joel stood up to approach Stephan who was chatting animatedly to the women about the night before. Daisy had almost forgotten that he too had ventured out into the clubs and pubs of Lincoln.

"Hi, I'm Joel," he offered his hand in greeting.

Stephan turned and shook hands with him, the pair eyed each other both ostensibly challenging the other to let go first. Daisy rolled her eyes and Georgie sniggered. Although Daisy considered that Stephan and Joel needed a proper introduction she decided that they did not deserve it. They could figure it out by having what women called a 'conversation'. Daisy ambled off to get dressed.

Last night, after Georgie had headed to bed, Joel had rambled on for far longer than necessary about how much he yearned for them to be a family again. Daisy just nodded and grunted in the right places, she knew that nothing of real substance could be discussed while Joel was so intoxicated. When he started to get sleepy she guided him up to her room so he could sleep it off. Once he started snoring Daisy crept back downstairs. She took the blanket off the back of the sofa and snuggled down. As tired as she had previously been the thoughts of Joel and her rekindling had played out in her mind. The images were primarily of her sat at home alone in the evening in the full knowledge that the only reason she was there with the children was so that he could venture out to visit his male friends, leaving her to babysit. Since having her own independence and conformation of his sexual orientation she could not return to the blissful ignorance of her former marriage.

Unlike him she no longer craved company, either his or otherwise. She had moulded her life into a full, satisfying one. She had weekends with her children to spend such as this one and then weekends where she socialised with other adults. Her evenings did not seem as empty as they had previously done because she had paperwork to do and having spent the day out and about with the dogs she appreciated relaxing at home. The pent-up, scared of the future Daisy had long gone. As far as Joel was concerned she was not his rock anymore, he had to sort his own life out.

She would always share a bond with him because they shared children and she would be amicable and friendly to make life as easy as possible for all involved. She would not, however, forfeit her happiness to fulfil his need for company and validation.

Later in the day, Daisy's surprise she entered the living room to see all five of them sat on the floor around the coffee table playing cards. Cory was teamed up with Stephan and Sally with Georgie, they were all determined to beat Joel. Snap seemed so much more complex with three sets of cards going down. No one could decide if they had to match two or three cards, it seemed to depend on who got which cards. Daisy sat in the armchair enjoying watching them all compete. The men seemed to be taking it more seriously than anyone else, as ever these occasions went.

Sally and Georgie won, which made all the males quite grumpy. Georgie being an old pro fetched the sweet snacks and fresh tea. After the frustration subsided, Daisy announced that they needed to start packing ready to go home. The children moaned, as was mandatory wherever they happened to be if they were having fun. They asked all the other adults in the room if they could come with them. Georgie and Stephan both explained that they couldn't and Joel agreed that he would meet them back at home. The children weren't happy with this decision and wanted to travel in his car. This offended Daisy, *why was she never the one they begged to spend time with?* Daisy felt like sulking but figured that it was better to channel her energy towards packing.

As always Daisy felt sad to be leaving the haven of Georgie's home. There was just the feeling of security and safety and as she drove home she felt as though she was heading off into unfamiliar territory, scared and naïve. It was at times like this that she seriously considered taking Joel up on his drunken offer of a reconciliation. But in her heart she knew that they would be the actions of two fearful adults clinging to the familiar rather than a responsible decision in the best interest of all involved. In reality life was good for her and the children, she had rebuilt her life and moulded it in a way she liked. The children seemed happy and she felt content most of the time. She put her current mindset down to the fact that she always got nervous about drive the distance home.

It could, however, be due to the farewell with Stephan who had stayed around to see them off. He had hugged her tight and kissed her affectionately on the cheek. Daisy had possibly enjoyed this embrace more than she should from a friend but as she clung to him she welled up and wanted nothing more than to melt into his embrace and never let go. Yet in her usual manner she simply pulled away and smiled and told him it had been great to see him again. They could now both return to the sanctuary of Facebook. To cry after Georgie hugged her was acceptable, if not expected. Joel had shook hands and the children had also given cuddles, Cory shook hands as well, wanting to mimic the grown up, man stuff.

She found herself yearning for Stephan, if only the children had managed to convince him to return home with them. He had thoroughly enjoyed the weekend with them. He was extremely good with the kids and enjoyed her company too. She was friends with his Aunt so they were practically family already. She formed an image in her mind of the four of them as a family and Georgie popping over for the weekend. She smiled through her tears.

"Mummy?" piped up Sally.

"Yes," she cleared her throat.

"Are you crying?"

Cory craned his head to try to see her in the rearview mirror.

"Yes," confirmed Cory before Daisy could answer.

"Why?" Sally asked.

"Because I miss my friends already," she cleared her throat again and changed the subject, she could not cry and drive it wasn't safe, "Did you have a nice weekend?"

"Yep," they chorused. And so the conversation flowed and her tears turned to happy smiles at the recollection of their activities. She was so pleased that they had liked Georgie and had fun. From what they had expressed, everyone had enjoyed themselves and Daisy vowed to do it again soon.

On their arrival home, Joel was already parked outside waiting for them. As soon as they stopped Daisy rubbed her eyes and Joel opened the car door for the children to jump out. She handed him the keys to unlock the front door.

"I'll put the kettle on," Joel announced.

"Cheers," she called, from the boot where she was retrieving all of their luggage.

As Joel made drinks and found biscuits, Daisy checked the phone messages and opened the post, writing messages on the envelopes as she went. There were three different messages from dog owners, two of whom were already clients and one was a prospective one. Apparently one of the dogs had been pining all weekend for her and they wondered if she was free to pop over and take Larry the poodle for a quick walk and fuss to settle him down. Daisy sighed, she loved her dog walking but seriously, some of the owners wanted her at their beck and call.

"Everything ok?" asked Joel as he passed her a strong coffee.

She rambled on for a few minutes about it, she needed to get it out of her system. She was fine after she got halfway down her mug.

"I'm so proud of you by the way."

Daisy hardly knew how to reply, "Thank you."

"No seriously, you are doing the most fantastic job with the children and your dog walking. I know, it is harsh to come home to the hassle of a poodle's emotional attachment issues but that means that they like you."

"I know." She ripped up the junk mail and threw it in the bin.

"I can watch the kids if you need to go and see Larry."

She contemplated his offer and decided to ring Larry's owner and take it from there.

Chapter Twenty-Eight- Male Rivalry

It was nice getting some air after the long drive home and in all honesty it was nice to be able to hand over for a change. She had done a couple of slow laps around the park and breathed in the warm air. While Joel was willingly sorting the kids out for bed she was happy to amble along with Larry gleefully bouncing alongside her. She approached the house and took a double take. She was sure that was his car but she was not overly good at spotting people's vehicles. *It definitely looked like his and who else could it be? What the hell was he doing here?* Her walking slowed as her brain sped up to try to sort out the information she was confronted with. She guessed she could ring his mobile and ask where he was. *But if he answered that he was at her house what would she do? She could run back and get Larry to take for another walk. God's sake this was stupid. It was her house.* She straightened her posture and strengthened her reprieve. She was going to walk into her house as though she hadn't even twigged it was his car, act as though it didn't bother her at all.

Daisy swanned through the front door, slipped her walking boots and coat off. As she attempted to look casual, relaxed and non-phased, she listened to see what it was that she was going into. The problem was that the house was eerily quiet. She strolled around the corner and the kitchen was empty. She switched on the kettle automatically, her ears still pricked for sounds of life. Hearing movement upstairs she made her way to see if the children had settled down alright. To her amazement Cory was fast asleep and Sally was laying contently in her bed just chatting to her teddy bear.

"Mummy, hello," she smiled widely, with a sleepy smile.

"Hi honey," she replied, giving her a huge hug.

They bidded each other goodnight and she nestled her back in.

After popping Cory a quick peck on the head she made her way back downstairs. The hum of conversation echoed through the kitchen, as she walked into the living room, Joel and Tristan were sat at ease, cups in hand chatting away like a couple of old ladies. It was a weird sight to see but not a comfortable one. The two significant men from her past were sitting here like a couple of friends. Daisy should technically have been reassured by this vision of amicability but then she was unsure as to whether Joel or Tristan knew who each other were. For all Joel knew Tristan was just a friend popping in to see her, and in reality that was all he was. But how Joel might feel if he knew that he was the long lost love of her life she did not know. And vice versa, did Tristan realise that Joel was her ex-husband, or just the good-looking gay babysitter.

They paused momentarily as she walked in and she offered them both a fresh drink.

"No I'm fine," they simultaneously replied.

Chills ran through her, she turned and went back to the kitchen, her refuge. While the kettle finished boiling, she just stood almost waiting for the reality of the situation to sink in. She tried to stretch the process as much as possible and leant against the worktop for a few seconds longer. Taking a deep breath she plastered a smile on her face and padded back to the living room. She had to remind herself that it was her house not Joel's. She sat herself comfortably the opposite end of the sofa to Joel, it was a split second decision, which side of the room did her loyalty lay.

Tristan met her eyes, she smiled, as did he. Joel seemed oblivious to the glance. Daisy's stomach jolted, the presence of Tristan in her house was warming. Part of her wished Joel would now just leave them to it. It sounded selfish, after him helping her with the children, but right here right now she wanted to be left to stare into his eyes. However, her sociable side kicked in and she joined in with their conversation. They were discussing the houses that Tristan had been looking at recently and bearing in mind that Joel had had to go through the same process they were well away putting the world to rights.

This was a comfortable subject, one that all of them were knowledgeable of. Tristan and Joel got on so well that Daisy almost forgot the background situation. It was a thoroughly enjoyable evening and Joel left around nine. Once he had, Daisy nipped to the toilet quickly, and Tristan offered to make them both a drink. She asked him what had brought him over here. He said that he had just left his Mum's and needed to chill out, and that it was becoming quite stressful with her being so ill and the hospital appointments were draining both him and her. Daisy felt sorry for him as he was still having to travel a lot of mileage to and from. Although from the earlier conversation he had a house in the pipelines that would hopefully sort as soon as possible. He did in fact look exhausted. Daisy would have been more than happy to pop him in her bed and wrap him up and let him rest. The thought made her blush and she brushed her fringe out of her eyes.

She was so comfortable in his company, and her mind wandered off towards the idea of them as a couple who would sit here every evening. She would make him hot chocolate and run him a big bubbly bath to settle him down after the stress of coping with his Mum. She could take homecooked meals over to her, to help her out, she had always got on well with his Mum. She was a wonderful lady and the idea of her being ill upset Daisy, even though she had not seen her for years. \she couldn't imagine how Tristan was feeling about this.

Although he was smiling and talking, there was a sadness behind his eyes. She wanted to walk across the short distance between them and hug him but his guard was up. She supposed that he probably cried alone at home or on the drive between the hospital and home. He looked as though he wanted nothing more than to stand and scream. To express his anger towards the illness that was sapping the life out of his once sprightly mother. The tiredness was starting to take its toll on him. Just in the last few weeks his skin looked paler and his eyes sunken, he had definitely lost weight; possibly just a couple of pounds or so but still it was noticeable, to those you bothered to look. Daisy wondered how many people did look past his charismatic smile, not many she guessed.

"Are you hungry? I was going to make some cheese on toast if you fancy some."

He momentarily looked like he was going to refuse but he accepted her offer with a grateful smile. He didn't have the energy to refuse. She quickly threw some together, it was lucky she hadn't offered him a sandwich because she had forgotten to get bread on the way home, thankfully she kept some in the freezer. She sprinkled Worcestershire sauce on the top as they were almost cooked and laid them out neatly on plates. She had done him four slices, he needed the energy.

As she walked into the living room she saw that he had fallen asleep. Quietly she placed the plates onto the coffee table. *Bless him. He really must be tired to have dropped off so quickly.* She fetched the blanket off the sofa and gently covered him over. He didn't so much as stir. Daisy took the two plates back to the kitchen and sat at the table eating her toasted cheese and skimming through Facebook. She was unsure whether to just leave him a note and go to bed or to wake him up and send him home. But it was such a long drive home for him and it was that drive which had left him so tired. She decided to leave him be for a while and just potter about and make a final decision just before she settled down for the night. The chances were he would wake up before then anyway.

In the end, Daisy had simply left him as he was and put a note on the coffee table next to him to say she had gone to bed. His face still looked strained as he slept, the stress staying with him even in his dreams. She was still unsure as to whether it had been the best plan of action, especially with her children in the house but she had felt too guilty to wake him. The children had not moved from where she had tucked them in. They looked so peaceful when they were asleep and she was so proud of the way they had behaved all weekend; not a bicker or an argument. It had been a confusing mix of events but Daisy had had a wonderful time.

Georgie had thoroughly enjoyed herself and the children had loved staying with her. The castle had been the daytrip of the year. Daisy smiled at the memory. Joel and Stephan had appeared to get on well and surprisingly the presence of either of them had not bothered anyone other than her. Even coming home to Joel and Tristan in her house had not been as bad a situation as she could ever had imagined. She got herself ready for bed and snuggled down with the book she had borrowed from Georgie. She was in no way racing through it but it was a nice way to relax occasionally, especially as she tried to resist cuddling up with Tristan while he looked so much like he needed the company. Her adversity to give off any of the wrong signals held her back from showing anything more than the basic friendly support. She didn't want to confuse either of them. She had to admit though that it was comforting having him here. Maybe she had to confess that having a man in the house still had the desired effect of comforting her sense of vulnerability.

Just as the words on the page were starting to blur there was a tap on her door. She sprung up expecting to see one of the children in need of the toilet.

"Sorry," Tristan apologised.

"It's ok, she reassured him, rubbing her eyes and moving her fringe out of them. She struggled to sit up.

"Don't get up, I can just lock the door and pop the keys back through."

"What time is it?"

"Late."

"You can't drive home at this time, stay till morning, get some rest."

"I would," he ran his fingers through his hair, "but I need to be up for work in the morning and I can't risk oversleeping. I have had to miss loads of time of work lately," he looked drawn again, he did not need to explain anything to her, she knew what he meant, "I'll be ok."

"If you are sure?" she climbed out of bed and into her dressing gown, the chill of the night making her shiver, "Promise you will text me when you get home please."

"Of course, I'm so sorry I fell asleep, I was really looking forward to that cheese on toast." He grinned.

"I can make you some now if you want," she stifled a yawn.

He touched her arm, "Don't be silly, I'll grab something on the way home, you need to sleep."

"Ok," she was not going to talk him in to it, mainly because she was too tired to.

She followed him down the stairs, being careful of her footing. They hugged goodbye briefly and she locked the door as soon as she saw he was safely in the car. After a quick nip to the toilet she curled back up in bed. To start with she didn't think she was going to be able to sleep but it took over instantaneously.

Chapter Twenty-Nine- Moody Monday

Monday morning hit with the usual intensity. The children screamed and argued while she tried to shower, milk got split all over the worktop. They refused to put on their uniforms and Daisy couldn't even find a clean top for herself and ended up fishing through the bag from Georgie's for the least smelly one. Luckily straight after the school run she was off to pick up Larry and two of his friends, and as much as dogs had a strong sense of smell they could not communicate to her how gross they thought she was.

Somehow they were out of the house on time. Daisy's heart-rate was at a dangerous level and the walk to school was no less calming. Sally and Cory managed to carry on their argument all the way to school. This was such a contrast to the weekend that Daisy just switched off from it, she was too upset by their behaviour that she just walked along with them and allowed them to just keep whinging, she felt that if she started to lay down the law she would lose her temper right now. Instead she knew that she just needed the stamina to get to school and run like hell once they were safely in the care of the teacher. Rarely did she feel like this but Lord, she was furious this morning. Maybe if she headed straight home and back to bed she could start again.

By the time she had walked to the houses to pick up the dogs her mood had lifted. She felt bad that she had not dealt with the children better but they had been so over the top, even for a Monday. She was sure that they would also have calmed down now they would be in assembly. She took a few more deep breaths, it really was a beautiful morning. She loved this time of the year, it was filled with the promises that she had seen on the train. The trees and plants were all now in full bloom and the world was renewed once more. She tried not to think about the fact that in just a couple of months the English weather would once more change; the sharpness of autumn, making everyone want to hibernate. Instead, she made the most of what was here now. As the dogs pulled on their leads, wanting to run around and be free, she smiled. This really was a blessed life that she was leading.

Her Mum rang her while she was sat on the log where she and Tristan had sat drinking coffee. She told her all about their weekend and promised her that they would take her when they visited the cathedral. Her Mum loved looking around old churches, so the cathedral would be much appreciated. She also loved the idea of the Bookstop Café. Her Mum told her all about her recent changes to the garden and about the living room that she had decorated in differing shades of browns. Talking to her Mum alleviated the final bubble of stress that Daisy had been holding on to and by the time she hung up she was unperturbed once more.

The dogs were having a whale of a time and watching them was amusing, they were so carefree and barked playfully at each other as they fought over sticks. Even as one of the regular dogwalkers passed by with her two german shepards, Daisy's dogs didn't batter an eyelid. The lady's dogs however were pulling at their leads keen to join in the fun. The two ladies acknowledged each other and commented on the weather as they usually did.

Her plan for socialising being part of her business had not emerged in quite the way she had hoped but she had still made many acquaintances. She was pleased about this and with her trips to Lincoln, visits with her Mum, the children and the three complicated men in her life, Daisy was happy to just pass the time of day with others. When her and the children had first embarked on the move, it had seemed such a life shattering experience that Daisy could not have foreseen that life would have turned out quite so well for them. She was from the generation of the nuclear family, so the single mother status had not seemed a positive one. But somehow, with good friends and family around her she had become quite strong. Managing the accounts, maintaining the house, scheduling the children and socialising had all become second nature and she reflected on why she ever felt the need to rely on a man.

She had to admit that she was actually a bit proud of herself and her accomplishments. Obviously, she was aware that compared to most people they were second nature but to a traditional wife, such as herself, they had felt like the scariest tasks in the world. Even the finances had worked out ok, luckily for her. Joel paid maintenance for the children and bought them clothing and shoes, and this eased the burden no end and she was immensely grateful for his assistance. The dogwalking was topping up the accounts quite nicely and she was handling her business accounts and filing without any mishaps.

The dogs returned to her when she called them, she clipped their leads back on and they meandered along back to each of their houses. She was in no hurry to get home today. Mainly because she knew that the wash pile was in need of her attention and she needed to go shopping. Two of her least favourite jobs. A small mercy was that because they had not been home all weekend the aftermath of the weekend was minimal. She texted Georgie just as she was arriving home to thank her for her hospitality. What with the emergency dog situation and the arrival of Tristan last night, Daisy had forgotten to text her. She replied straight away expressing her enjoyment of the visit and said that she hoped they came again soon. Daisy replied, telling her about the idea of taking her Mum to see the cathedral soon. She might do this visit without the children as they had not seemed overly enthusiastic to see it. The c was of the most interest to them. Daisy knew that Mum and Georgie would get on really well, in fact, Georgie and her Mum were very similar in character. That was probably why they had hit it off from the word go.

When she picked the children up from school Sally told her that her teacher had been so interested in her diary entry about Lincoln castle that they were planning some class topic work on it. Daisy was pleased that she had enhanced her children's education, even if it had been in a round about way. Cory on the other hand was very quiet.

"What's wrong honey?"

"Nothing?"

"You sure?"

"Yep." He kept his head down and he was in no way ok. Daisy allowed him time to chill down on the walk home; she would ask him again later. Cory with his excitable character was sometimes mistaken for being as tough as nails. But in reality he was a sensitive little soul. All it took sometimes was the slightest comment or action by someone and he would be upset for days.

It transpired later that evening that a couple of the boys in his class had teased him about his Dad being gay. Cory pleaded with her not to tell the teacher but Daisy told him that this was one promise she could not keep, the teacher needed to be made aware. The chances were that they were just being mean and didn't actually know that his Dad was really gay, it was just one of those words that kids threw around. Yet she was not going to let it pass. She hugged Cory and explained her thoughts on the teasing; he seemed reassured by this and perked up a bit. Children could be so cruel and most of the time not even realise the damage they do. Schools could sh environment and she did not want her bad experience, especially this young. They school to survive yet.

Georgie rang her in the evening very excited.

"I booked it," she exclaimed.

"Booked what?"

"The Ann Summers party. At least five people from the coffee mornings wanted to come and I figured you and your Mum could join in too. You said she wanted to visit the cathedral."

"Yes I did, but I'm not sure the two activities should be rolled into one weekend, God might not approve."

Georgie burst out laughing, "He won't mind," she reassured her. "That does land on Joel's weekend doesn't it?" she asked in her serious voice.

"Yes, you got it right. I'll ring my Mum and see if she's up for it."

Georgie continued laughing.

"Oh, Georgie, you have such a dirty mind, all this Ann Summers stuff is messing with your head." This caused Georgie to laugh even harder.

They rang off and Daisy called her Mum quickly while helping the children into their pyjamas. Surprisingly she was quite excited by the prospect.

"I haven't been to one of those in years; it was more Tupperware parties in my day. How fun!"

"Excellent, I'll let Georgie know to count us in."

The return phonecall to Georgie to book them in involved lots more cackling on Georgie's part about Tupperware and dildos. Daisy laughed but could not join in too much as little ears were still listening. They were now at the teeth cleaning part of the bedtime routine so Daisy left Georgie to her crudeness and set off to find the children's bedtime book.

The kettle had hardy started boiling for her post-bedtime-routine-coffee when the phone rang. She was tempted to ignore it but she knew that curiosity would get the better of her.

"Hello."

"Hi Daisy, it's Tristan." He voice sounded strained, "I wondered if you would mind if I popped over."

"Sure," she checked her appearance in the mirror as she spoke. Hopefully she'd have time for a shower and tidy up.

"Cool, I'm just leaving the hospital, see you in a minute."

Shit. "Ok."

She quickly dragged the hairbrush through her hair and cleaned her teeth. By the time she had got an extra cup out of the cupboard he was tapping on the door. She was concerned for him when she saw how much more exhausted he looked in just one day. It transpired that he had got halfway home that morning and the hospital had called. He had spent the day at his mother's bedside, on only the short sleep he had had at hers. She rubbed his arm to comfort him and tears instantly sprang to his eyes. She paused before pulling him in and allowing him to cry on her shoulder.

His sobs shook through his entire body as she held him tight and allowed him to release the emotions that had been required to be held on to in order to support his mother. She found herself wanting to cry too but did not let go, she needed her to be tough for him. The minutes passed and gradually his tears dried and his body calmed, she released her grip. When he finally pulled away from her his head was held low and he slowly raised it and his sad eyes met hers.

"I'm so sorry, I don't know where that came from."

"It's ok, it needed to come out. Coffee?"

"Please." He pulled out a chair to sit down, his body was weak from fatigue.

She placed their beverages on the table between them and fetched a packet of bourbons. Neither one of them spoke for a moment and to start with all Tristan could do was apologise. She reassured him that it was perfectly fine and thought about how much she wished she had been able to break down on someone's shoulder. But other than her Mum no one else had ever really seen her cry since Joel and her broke up. She had talked to people but only her nearest and dearest. In all fairness until she had met Georgie it had been a long time since she had confided in anyone. Daisy found it hard to just let rip and not double think everything she was saying and assess whether it would upset or offend them. With Georgie, who had not known any of her family or friends, she had been able to open up fully and in return Georgie had shared her woes.

As much as Daisy did not really want a 'relationship' with Tristan she knew that he needed her. If nothing else she was happy to be his sounding board or confidant. His presence was most welcome in fact, again as she had the last night, she felt calm with him here. She was uncertain why he would have this effect on her. Possibly it was because they were so familiar with each other's true selves; the people they were when they were young, before the world had tarnished them. It could have been the fact that he made her feel young again, maybe it was because he looked at her as though he could see straight into her soul and feel the longing in her heart for love and acceptance. Then again, maybe she was just sympathising with him during this traumatic time.

Chapter Thirty- Teddy Bears Picnic

Daisy was surprised to receive the invitation to Tristan's new house. She was mostly surprised by the fact he invited the children too. Sally was slightly apprehensive. She liked going out to lunch, and after having had tea at Georgie's she was hoping that it might be the same set up but she shared her concerns with Daisy about the lack of cake and 'proper' tea. Daisy asked her why she thought he might not do the same as Georgie.

"Because he's a man," was her simple reply. Sally scrunched up her nose as she said it and it took all of Daisy's reserve not to burst out laughing. Instead she simply nodded in agreement and turned to smirk.

The children ran around the house collecting up teddies, colouring book and pens, DSs and games. Daisy thought she even saw a few other random items go into their bags such as ninjas, and half the doll house furniture.

As the put their rucksacks into the car, Sally ran back get her favourite hat; a white crocheted beanie with a Daisy on the front.

"Sweetheart, you do know it is 25 degrees today don't you?"

"Please let me wear it, I love it, it's my favourite."

Daisy agreed, mainly to not start an argument, but also because she looked far too cute to question her fashion decisions. Cory passed his CD choice through to her.

"Pl… ea… se."

Daisy smiled wide at his choice. Coldplay had always been his favourite. As a baby it had made him sleepy. Even now would doze off to it.

"I won't fall asleep, don't worry." Daisy smiled wide, these kids were on top form today.

They drove through town and pulled into Tristan's driveway. The door opened as she pulled on the handbreak. He stood with his hands in his pockets and his shoulders practically up by his ears. He had a tight smile on his face. Daisy knew this stance; he was nervous, very nervous. The seatbelts came off, the bags were fetched and the children climbed out. They stood in front of him, waiting for directions as to what to do next. Daisy locked the car and as she strolled over to them, he stepped down and kissed her on the cheek. Instantly they all relaxed and he greeted the children and led them all into the house.

"I'm so glad you came."

"Me too, thank you for inviting us." He looked good, tired but good.

"Would you like the TV on for them?"

"No, they're ok, thanks. Is it ok to set them up to do some drawing at the table?"

"Erm, yes they are welcome to draw, but the table might be a problem."

Daisy was confused, maybe he had set it up ready for tea. She turned round to check. The place was sparse and apart from a sofa, a side table with a lamp on it and a few cardboard packing boxes in the corner, the place was empty. Daisy blushed at her presumptuousness.

"Sorry, I hadn't realised you didn't have one."

He touched her arm, "Honestly, it is fine. Are they ok to sit on the floor to draw?"

"Yea, of course." By the time they had discussed the set-up, the children were both settled onto their DSs.

"Problem solved," Daisy jested. "So anything I can do to help?"

"Erm," he glanced around the kitchen, almost double checking, "No, think it is all under control. Are they ok with ham sandwiches and cake?"

"Perfect. Thank you for doing this for us."

"Seriously, please relax, it is no bother. I thought we could all do with a bit of time to chill out."

Daisy smiled widely at him, and their eyes met for a second. Daisy flushed. She averted he eyes and started rummaging in her bag for her phone. She was unsure what exactly she was checking it for but she needed to stop feeling these conflicting thoughts about Tristan.

"Right here you go kids," Tristan unfolded a blanket and laid it on the living room floor. "Make yourselves comfy."

The children laid their DSs to one side and crawled giggling on to it. Sally set to pulling her teddies out of her bag. She chatted to them as she did so, explaining to them where they were and what they were going to do. Cory sat cross-legged and watched Sally, patiently waiting for the teddies to be seated. Daisy moved to help gather the plates of food but Tristan gently steered her towards the blanket. She complied, she had always liked the way he gently took charge. It had never been overly dominating or authoritive, as some people were, but somehow soothing.

Daisy joined the children on the blanket and they all grinned widely at each other. Daisy fleetingly wondered if this would have been how they would have spent their weekends if they had stayed together and raised their own family. She imagined it could have been and a twinge of nostalgia for something she would or could never actually know ran through her. She had played the 'what if' game now and then, sometimes wondering how different decisions would have impacted her life and the way it had turned out. It was never tinged with regret, more intrigue.

What if Joel and her had never gone past the first couple of dates? What if her and Trstan had got married and had a family? What if things had never gone so bad in the beginning, how would life be now? Would they have gone the distance? In all fairness she had to admit to herself that most of her 'what ifs' involved Tristan. Mainly because he had been the big love of her life, and if it had been a movie they would have made it and had the happy ending.

"Are you ok Mummy?" Cory asked. Snapping her out of her thoughts Daisy realised she was crying, silently, just a couple of tears running down her cheeks. She wiped them away and gave the lame excuse of something in her eye. Whether the children believed her or not, she did not know.

Tristan laid the plates of food in the middle of the blanket and handed round floral paper plates and matching napkins. He had obviously not been quite as spontaneous as he appeared to have been. Daisy melted a little inside at the effort he had put in. He just kept surprising her. For so many years the image in her head of him was far detached from the man she saw in front of her as he served her children sandwiches, cakes and fizzy juice. The smile on his face was genuine and the children reacted accordingly. Daisy stood to lean against the doorway to the living room and just observed the wonderfully 'Kodak' moment in front of her. A lump appeared in her throat and she had to swallow hard to stop herself from bursting into tears.

Tristan turned and stood up from where he had been kneeling so as to assist the bears with their sandwich eating. Sally and Cory giggled away as this burly man served tea to their toys. He smiled at her and his eyes held her gaze. She wanted nothing more than to embrace him and never let him go. *Reserve yourself, Daisy, nothing good ever came from following your heart.* However, as she deliberated this for a moment, her children and her history with Tristan had actually created a fabulous life which, all things considered, had worked out quite well.

She stepped aside to let him pass through the doorway. The hairs on her arms stood as his aura brushed past hers; the recognition of an entity it had known so well. It felt as though her soul instantaneously sprung to attention at him being at such close proximity. Her breath caught and it took all her reserve not to gasp out loud. Cory broke her from her dream-like state as he called her over to join them.

"Of course, sorry," she stumbled over the words, fighting the inner battle against her raw emotions and reality. Reality had to win at this moment in time, because torturing herself with past 'what ifs' was a losing battle in itself. She knew she had to be strong and not fall for the classic games played in order to participate in a relationship with others. She knew that she was over analysing the situation but after the initial declaration of feeling for her and longing to right past wrongs she needed to be on her guard. She also realised, which caused her to smirk, that Joel's obsession with war films had installed in her many battle analogies.

Sitting cross-legged on the blanket not only caused her muscles to go dead after a few minutes but also it was a lovely way to spend the afternoon. Tristan really did have a naturally good manner with children and the teddies were included in this. Daisy excused herself to pop to the toilet just before they started on the cakes.

She glanced at her reflection in the bathroom mirror. Her eyes were greener than normal, a sign that she was in 'witchy' mode, her mother used to say, maybe she was; possibly trying to suss the situation out. It was hard of course because she was judging him by past experience, not taking into account the fact that he might have changed. But her dilemma was that she was unsure whether she wanted him to have changed. All things aside she had loved him more deeply than she knew was possible. The past events had not stopped her loving him but had simply diluted her feelings and tested her trust. To her at that point in time it had been enough for her to run and hide, and resulted in her falling into the arms of a man who had loved her but never eliminated her feeling for Tristan. As the thought hit her she gasped and her hand flew to her mouth. *Was it true? Had her marriage to Joel simply been a safe haven against her love for Tristan?*

Daisy stood staring into the mirror, a sudden feeling of upset washed over her and the tears began to fall almost before she realised she was upset. Puzzlingly though she was unsure as to why she felt this overwhelmingly emotional. She closed her eyes, hugged her arms around herself and just stood, eyes closed, her breathing heavy, gasping through the sobs. It was at this moment that the realisation hit her. She had missed something. No someone. An important time or person had passed her by somewhere during her life. Her heart yearned as though the person had moved too far from her reach. She opened her eyes to see her reflection staring back at her. Her reflected eyes questioned her, willing her to remember, who and where and why. An image of Tristan flashed before her mind's eye and her heart quickened. She stared back and acknowledged what her unconscious had needed her to remember, her mind had thrown the emotion and image of the loss of Tristan from her life into the forefront of her memory. Some would call it a 'wake-up' moment, some an epiphany. Whatever it was it had woken her up to her true inner feelings for Tristan. No more 'go with the flow', this was time to take action. Even if he rejected her, like she had rejected him there on the riverside, she had to get these feelings out of her head and heart and tell him. What happened then, who cared, she needed him to know, no matter what the consequences.

The knock on the door stopped her dropping to the floor in an emotional heap. She splashed her face, trying not to smudge her mascara, not an easy feat. Fake smile back on her face she took one last glance at her reflection. She could not look any better right now.

"Look Mummy," Sally held the teddy out to show her Mum. Daisy's legs gave up fighting for stability, she dropped to the floor. Tristan came running through, Cory at his heels. Nothing needed to be said, Tristan knew. Her bright green eyes held his this time, the greenness was unmistakeable. Tristan went pale and Sally dropped the teddy to her side, her eyes filling with tears.

"Sorry," he mouthed to her.

Daisy hugged Sally to reassure her that she had done nothing wrong. Then she looked back at Tristan. The look spoke volumes. Wordless questions and actuations flew in his directions. *How the hell did he still have the teddy?* She scooped up the children and they left. They were obviously confused as to why they didn't stay for cake but Daisy needed to get away. She had told Tristan that her Mum had called and they needed to go. She knew that he knew better as he put the cakes on a plate with cling film on it for them. Daisy apologised to the children as they drove home, but her voice was thick with emotion and her head was spinning. In all fairness she knew that she needed to pull herself together in order to function and drive safely. Yet she felt as though she had let herself down by allowing her defences to come down.

The wind blew through the open window as they were almost home. *Let it go.* Daisy shivered as though someone had just whispered in her ear. She breathed deep. *Yes.* She silently answered back. The feeling of understanding and reassurance washed over her and she allowed the pent up feeling to disperse.

Chapter Thirty-One - The Ann Summers Experience

It had been a few weeks since Daisy had seen Stephan, they Facebooked each other but they had both drifted back into their separate worlds. In all honesty, she had been too busy with her dogs, children and Tristan to notice. It was not until she was on her way to Lincoln with her Mum that she thought about it. She considered the concept that he might be seeing someone or that the awkward encounters of her last visit had made him pull back from their friendship. She had obviously been right in her initial analysis of their relationship: he was stunningly gorgeous and young, she was not; friends was all they would ever be. She decided right there and then as she drove her way down the A17 that she would enjoy their flirting but remember not to read too much into it. She could still dream about him but in her own time.

"So," her Mum broke her out of her own thoughts, "tell me more about your friend Georgie."

Daisy was pleased to change the subject in her mind and filled her Mum in on all the details of Georgie and her life. She retold the story of how they met in the breakfast room of the hotel after the reunion and then how her nephew had turned out to be the angel barman. *There she was back on the subject of Stephan.* She mentally reprimanded herself and shared her concerns of Georgie and her relationship with her daughter. Daisy's Mum was a fantastic listener, she would make all the right noises in all the right places and then when the person had finished she would reply with the most profound prognosis.

"It sounds to me as though Georgie just needs a good friend to share her life with and that there are obviously issues that stem from long ago. A lot of the time a child becoming a parent changes their perspective of themselves and the interplay of their relationships with others. Such as how Georgie's daughter was raised or treated may differ immensely from how she brings up her child. This leads to a differing of opinion and also criticism of her mother's parenting skills."

"Oh, that makes sense." Daisy pondered over whether she had felt like this when she had become a mother, although she valued her Mum's opinion of parenting because she had felt her Mum had done a good job. If anything she aimed to be as much like her as was possible. She rang her Mum about any issues regarding the children or in fact anything from recipes of pastry to plants to yoga positions that relieve period pains. She guessed she was lucky, she idolised her Mum. Georgie's daughter for whatever reason did not. Her Mum was right, as ever, she needed to just be a good friend to Georgie; it was not her job to try to fix Georgie's relationship with her daughter.

"I'm very excited about tonight's gathering by the way," her mum blurted out.

Daisy laughed; partially from shock but mainly with amusement. Her Mum was so fun to be around, full of zest for life. Daisy hoped to one day be as optimistic as her or at least a little bit less 'woe be me'. She knew that as of recent years her life had been an unhappy one but still her Mum's life had not been all smooth sailing either. Yet here she was bouncing around like a child on a day trip to the zoo. Daisy smiled.

"Me too Mum." She placed her hand gently over her mother's, "I'm so glad you have come, it will be a really good night."

Her Mum was positively beaming as she watched the countryside pass by. She still pointed out livestock and farm machinery as she had done when Daisy was little. She was unsure if this was purely for her own pleasure or out of habit. Either way Daisy liked it, it made her feel comforted, looked after somehow.

"Oh, how is that lovely young Tristan doing these days?"

"Erm, yea not too good with his Mum being so ill but we spend quite a lot of time together. It takes his mind off things and gives me some company. I like it when he walks with me while I'm taking out the dogs."

"Such a shame about his Mum, she is a lovely lady. Perhaps it would be nice if I went to see her, we used to get on really well back when…" her words drifted off, almost as though she had put her foot in it but more like she missed the old days. Tristan's parents and hers had been close, regular coffees and visits to each other's houses. Just like families of couples should be. Yet after Daisy and Tristan split it made the situation uncomfortable for everyone. Over the years they had met up for coffee but it drifted off, much like her mother's words had done. It was a shame. Daisy missed those days too. Daisy and Tristan had chatted briefly about the time they were a couple. But neither one of them wanted to confess in detail to having yearned for it in the way they both had. It was a matter of self-preservation. To admit regret would mean mistakes had been made, and they both knew that their relationship had well and truly run its course.

Georgie and Helena hit it off straight away, there had never been a doubt in Daisy's mind that they would. Daisy sat back watching the pair of them, acting as though they had known each other a lifetime. Daisy took the time to doze in the chair, it had been a long week and a long drive and it had caught up with her. She knew that although having Tristan around was nice, his needs were great right now and sometimes Daisy felt drained after he left. However, she was willing to allow him to take some of her energy if it helped him get through this time with his mother. The poor man was exhausted.

He had now moved closer, he was renting a cottage just a few roads away from his parent's home. It was sparse and he had not had the time to make it home.

She doubted he would stay there long after his mother's inevitable passing, it would hold too many memories. Daisy considered where it would leave her, not in a selfish way so much as in a curious, 'would she be a connection to the bad memory' sort of way.

She awoke an hour or so later, slightly dazed and to the sound of excited chatter in the other room. Someone had placed a blanket over her and the curtains had been drawn to dim the room. *No wonder she had slept.* Daisy started getting tired if she put on sunglasses, any slight hint of darkness struck the melatonin in her brain on to overdrive. She gradually eased her body upright, she had not realised just how tired she had been.

The two ladies turned to greet her as she entered the kitchen.

"There's fresh coffee in the pot honey."

"Excellent, thank you." She went to pass them and into the bathroom when she caught sight of the computer. "What the hell are you two up to now?" She felt as though she was reprimanding her kids again, "I can't leave you alone for two minutes."

The two women cackled and looked rightfully shameful.

"We were doing research," Georgie replied defensively.

"On what?" Daisy realised her voice had gone up at least two octaves.

Daisy's Mum was blushing but with a huge grin on her face.

"Well," Georgie had managed to stop smirking, well just about, "Toms."

Daisy's Mum went into a fit of giggles again while Georgie held on tight to her amusement. Daisy however was less reserved.

"Oh my God Georgie, what are you doing to my poor mother?"

"It was her idea."

At that, Daisy shot a look of horror at her Mum and ran to the bathroom. *Ok, so she had told her Mum about the Tom scenario but she had not gone so far as to Google it! Maybe bringing her Mum was not such a good idea, this was mortifying.*

The aged computer had been switched off and the equally aged women were now sat looking forlorn, awaiting their fate, coffees in hand. Daisy simply poured herself a coffee and turned to face them both.

"We found out that Tom comes in many different shapes and sizes depending on one's needs," her Mum spoke quite matter-of-factly about it.

"I'm sure they do Mum but we need to leave something for the Ann Summers lady to talk to us about, I don't think they give you a test on your knowledge."

"I know Dear but luck favours the prepared." Helena's solemn face broke into a smirk again and Daisy had to join Georgie in her cackling.

"Oh Mum, I think you are taking this far too seriously."

"Sweetheart, I think it may be you taking it too seriously." She winked at Daisy and Daisy playfully huffed at her.

"Now, now children, play nice," Georgie jested.

The doorbell rang to break up the moment.

"Yay, people are here," announced Georgie, as though they would not have known from the doorbell chiming.

"Daisy, Helena, this is Francine and Elizabeth. Two of my dear friends from the coffee mornings." They all swapped greetings with each other and as Daisy nipped off to freshen up, the four ladies could be heard discussing the findings of their research. Daisy simply rolled her eyes at the whole thing. She determined that no matter how old she got, taking her Mum to an Ann

Summers party might not have been the best idea. She considered ringing Stephan to see if he fancied going out for the night instead, leave the oldies to it but felt that it would be letting the side down. She tried to convince herself that it would be fine, the evening would be fun. If nothing else she knew where Georgie kept the alcohol.

By the time Daisy reappeared downstairs three more ladies, Jane, Hayley, Edwina, along with Debbie, the Ann Summers lady had arrived. The women were acting as though it was sale day at Marks & Spencer, grabbing at the items in the bag before poor old Debbie could get them out to display. The screeching and giggling was contagious and while Daisy helped herself to a glass of wine and some nibbles she found herself sniggering too.

They were a fabulous bunch and women and Daisy now saw just why Georgie had chosen this group to share the night with. Daisy's Mum was up there with the best of them, commenting and laughing. A couple of times Daisy had to mentally switch off to the fact that she was her daughter, as stories and experiences were eagerly swapped. If Daisy had thought that old age would bring about boredom, her opinion had certainly changed. These ladies were not only extremely funny but apparently quite sexually experienced. To say that she was shocked was an understatement.

Debbie was very serious about her job which amused everyone even more. Every time a story was regaled or a dildo was laughed at Debbie cleared her throat and pulled a 'teacher-like' expression. Georgie seemed to be deliberately testing her. Just as Debbie pulled out the dildo resembling the one that Georgie herself had purchased, Georgie jumped up and grabbed it, cuddled it and started explaining the 'Tom' thing. Daisy nearly spat her drink all over the rail of lingerie. Debbie was practically coughing up her lungs, trying to bring the room back to order. But the more she coughed the more everyone laughed and the conversation no longer had words in as much as noises. Tears were running down their cheeks and Debbie was getting redder and redder. Daisy was concerned that Debbie was going to burst something.

Just as Hayley had disappeared off to dress in a sexy cheerleader outfit, Daisy's phone rang in her bag. She quickly scooped it up, relieved to be able to leave the room, and ran to the kitchen to answer it. It was Tristan.

Chapter Thirty-Two- Saved By The Bell

Daisy stood in the kitchen, her mobile to her ear and her other hand attempting to block out the racket going on in the other room.

"Hello," she shouted in to the phone.

It was silent for a second and then Tristan spoke. "She's gone," was all he could muster.

Daisy's hand flew from her ear to her mouth. The noise penetrated her eardrum and hit her as hard as the news. *Shit!*

"Tristan, I'm in Lincoln at the moment but I will get back as soon as I can tomorrow morning. I can't leave yet as I've been drinking, I'm so sorry." Her head was spinning. *Typically, one of the few times she had gone away and couldn't get back!* Her brain went into overtime trying to work out a possible way that she could get home to him. *He was understandably devastated. How could she not be there for him.*

"You are welcome to come here if you want," she said into the silent receiver, "but I'm worried about you driving under the circumstances."

There was a grunt or a sob, it was hard to make out the difference. She really had no idea what to do. Hayley came can-canning through the kitchen, pom-poms flying. The screams and cheers from the women was deafening. Instinctively Daisy shushed her, her finger over her lips. She scuttled further from the noise and into the bathroom.

"Tristan, are you ok? I'm so worried about you."

"I'll be ok. I'll see you tomorrow." He hung up. She knew he was not being off with her, he was in shock. She didn't want him to be alone. She wanted to run to him. To hug him, to reassure him that everything would be alright; except it wouldn't be alright. His mother had died. Obviously, she was no longer in pain but she was also no longer with him. Daisy could not imagine how it must feel to lose a parent, she had been very lucky. But for Tristan this was his only parent since his Dad had died many years before. She had been his rock and he had been hers. As she sat in the bathroom she felt overwhelmed with grief. In her mind's eye she saw Tristan floating in a stormy sea, alone and distressed and most strongly came through the idea that he was lost; without direction. He had nowhere to aim. She saw herself as the lighthouse and from somewhere deep inside her she sent him out a beacon and wrapped him in the bright light. For now, until he found salvation elsewhere she would be his saving grace.

At this moment in time it was the best that she could do, after three glasses of wine there was no chance that she was going drive home. She stood up with a sense of determination. She dried her eyes and made her way back towards the gaggle of gals. The sight that met her was unexpected. There in the middle of the room dressed as a sexy nurse was her Mum, Hayley the cheerleader was spelling out her name and Georgie was chasing her with Tom. There was nothing more Daisy could do than burst out laughing. What a way to snap her out of her desperate and helpless mood. Well, for now, she figured there was nothing much she could do so she may as well enjoy the party. She grabbed Tom from Georgie and chased her back with him, one hand on her hip, thrusting and waving it at her like a sword. The women laughed even harder and Debbie had sat herself down behind her rail of lingerie with a glass of red.

Whether or not Debbie was amused by the antics was neither here nor there as she had most certainly made her quota for the week on this party alone. They all ordered some version of Tom and a fun outfit. By the end of the night Debbie was rosy cheeked and smiling. It was hard to tell if it was the effect of the wine and the relief that the party was finally over, but either way they had all had the most wonderful time.

It was well after mid-night when the last guest left and Georgie, Daisy and Helena sat around the kitchen table complaining about how much their stomachs and cheeks hurt from all the laughing. It was obviously good-natured moaning as they had thoroughly enjoyed themselves. Daisy watched her Mum and Georgie and was extremely pleased that the two of them were getting on so well, if anything they had more in common than her and Georgie. Seeing her Mum enjoying herself, smiling and laughing had pleased Daisy, her Mum deserved to relax.

Mid-conversation Helena suddenly asked her who had phoned. In all honesty Daisy had forgotten Tristan's phonecall, the shock of her mother's shenanigans had pushed it from her mind. The sadness washed over her again, just as the doorbell rang.

"Lord, who forgot what? I do hope Hayley didn't leave her underwear behind."

Daisy and her Mum exchanged an amused look. Georgie made it sound like quite a regular event. But as she re-entered the room Daisy flew from her seat. There stood Tristan, puffy eyed and looking like the boy she had first fallen in love with. She wrapped her arms around him and the other two ladies nipped past them, allowing them the time they needed alone.

Tristan melted into her arms, he didn't cry, he just held onto her as though he had travelled the world in search of her. The energy between the two of them was intense; that of soul-mates being reunited after lifetimes apart. They connected on a level far beyond human comprehension. Daisy was unsure how long they had stood there but when they finally parted, mainly due to Georgie being in desperate need of the toilet, Daisy led him by the hand up to the spare bedroom. Her Mum was sleeping in the room the children had shared, so

Daisy guided him to lay on the bed in the other room, like an exhausted child. She slipped off his shoes and jacket, and simply covered them both with the duvet. They both fell into a deep sleep wrapped in the safeness of each other.

Daisy slipped out of bed early the next morning, leaving Tristan to sleep. Sleep was healing, or so they said. He was in definite need of both. The last few months had taken their toll on him and it still wasn't over. The grieving process was a long one. She sat in the kitchen, her hands cupped around her mug, staring at a stain on the wall, while her mind ran around crazily trying to figure out her next move. She knew that she needed to be careful to protect her own feelings for Tristan. As a friend she knew that he needed her, but the energy between them last night could not be dismissed. She needed to think rationally, to be there to support him yet not allow things to evolve between them until he was in a better place within himself. *Easier said than done.*

"Good morning," Georgie greeted her.

"Oh, morning," replied Daisy slightly dazed.

"You ok?" enquired Georgie as she busied herself making coffee.

"Erm, yea, I'm ok thanks."

"Really, you seem a tad troubled." She spooned in the sugar.

Daisy gave a half smile.

"Come on, a problem shared and all that…"

Daisy explained, semi-aware of the fact that Tristan could appear at any moment. Georgie simply listened and sipped her coffee allowing Daisy to just open up. She had seen the pair of them together and how well they connected. From an older, supposedly wiser perspective she could see that they were destined to be together. However, she was also aware that there were far greater issues that were keeping the two of them apart. Possibly, she thought, they would work through the shadows of the past that were holding them at a distance. Yet as Daisy spoke openly she could see the fear and concern for the feelings she had for him and now she didn't want this vulnerability he was feeling at the present time to bring them together for all the wrong reasons. As Georgie had seen before, the shadows of one's past rear their ugly heads eventually, and normally at the most inconvenient of times.

"Morning," greeted a sleepy Helena.

"Morning," Daisy and Georgie replied simultaneously.

"I feel like I drunk a little bit too much wine," she grimaced, running her fingers through her hair.

Daisy shook off the feeling of discontent and Georgie tried to pull her mind back from her own turbulent past. Both ladies smiled at the recollection of the previous night's events. Daisy's Mum made a pot of coffee.

When Tristan finally appeared the mood had cleared and Daisy had put her mind to rest. She had decided to just 'go with the flow', something she was not very good at if the truth be told. However, she had learned that worrying and stressing solved nothing other more than causing stress and worry. After her little prep-talk with Georgie and her Mum, she had come to the conclusion that time was a healer in many different ways. There may, of course, be hope that her and Tristan might start dating, but at this moment in time, his mother's funeral and helping him through his grieving process were the priority. Possibly it was seeing him at his darkest moment that had brought out her nurturing side; maybe she still loved him. Maybe what they had previously shared was all they were destined to share. She didn't know. All she could be sure about at this moment in time was that he needed her more than ever to just be a supportive friend. So 'go with the flow' she would. Any questions could wait till later.

Chapter Thirty-Three- Back To Reality

Arriving home after dropping her Mum off, Daisy kicked off her shoes, switched on the kettle and sunk into the sofa. It had been a long tedious drive home, lots of caravans heading to the coast, unsure of the right direction to go in. But she was home now and Tristan had text her to say he had also arrived home safe. She figured that he was obviously better at overtaking than her; in that she only overtook static vehicles or very slow tractors. She heard the kettle switch itself off but was too lethargic to move. The emotional turmoil of Tristan's visit had left her feeling even more drained. She knew that it was selfish of her to even contemplate her own feelings but at this moment she was going to allow herself to stop. She pulled the blanket from the back of the sofa and curled up, instantly falling asleep.

The sound of the phone woke her and she sleepily aimed in the general direction of it. As ever it stopped just as she picked up. She gave a deep sigh and re-boiled the kettle while dialling 1471. It was Joel. She glanced at the clock, she had slept for two hours. *Opps.* She rang him back, the phone cradled in the crook of her neck, and made the coffee.

"Sorry I just missed you, what's up?" she held her breath, hoping everything was alright with the children.

"Oh nothing, I tried your mobile too, I was wondering if you were still in Lincoln actually."

"Erm no, I got back a couple of hours ago, why?" she could feel herself frowning.

"We are heading up there in a bit and the kids asked if we could meet you for dinner if you were." He sounded quite nonplussed.

"That would have been lovely, sorry." She felt quite disappointed that she had missed the opportunity to see the children, even though they would be home later that evening.

"No worries, I'll let them know, we'll plan ahead next time."

"Ok, send them my love."

"Will do, bye."

He had rung off before she had a chance to question why they were going to Lincoln. *Hmm, how strange. Obviously the children were enjoying their visits to Lincoln and if that was where they thought she was they might have asked to go. Bless them, how sweet.*

Daisy sipped her coffee, her blanket still wrapped around her and returned to the sofa. She was at a loss now. She fancied going for a walk, although it felt odd to do it without the dogs. Maybe she could ask to borrow one for a couple of hours. *That would be really sad.* Instead she text Tristan to ask if he'd like to join her. *So much for 'going with the flow'.*

Chapter Thirty-Four- Facing Your Demons

Throughout the summer Georgie and Daisy met regularly. Usually Daisy visited her, sometimes the children or her Mum would join her. In all fairness Georgie and Helena's friendship had also blossomed into a wonderfully jovial affair. Daisy should probably have been jealous that her friendship had been compromised yet she actually felt it enhanced her relationship with both ladies. Also the fact that they both had more free time on their hands meant that it was nice for them to have someone to share daily antics with. Daisy had an overwhelming feeling that in reality her chance meeting with Georgie all those weeks ago had been in order for her to subsequently meet Helena. The pair of them had been in need of companionship for longer than they would have ever admitted. She guessed it was probably a similar case to that of her and Tristan in that she hadn't realised she had been missing anything in her life until he had arrived and showed her the attention she had in fact been craving.

It was the fourth of July and the annual airshow was being held at RAF Waddington. Daisy had promised the children that they would attend and Helena had chosen to join them. Daisy was pleased that she was because sometimes when she was out and about with the children she needed an extra pair of hands and authorative voice to keep them in check. Not to say they were unruly but the excitement got too much at times. Georgie was going to meet them there and was extremely excited about the prospect of men in uniform. It seemed to Daisy that there was a distinct possibility that it was Georgie who would be in need of supervision.

Daisy had not realised just how popular these events were until she had been sat in the queue of traffic for an hour and a half. Finally they managed to park and dragged themselves from the stuffy car. Her t-shirt was stuck to her back. It was at times like this that she wished for a car with air-conditioning. Daisy's Mum was stretching out her back and the children were having one last rummage in the food bag. This pleased her because the refreshments at these things were always so expense.

The atmosphere was fantastic, everyone was smiling and chatting and excited. Out from the crowd emerged Georgie equally as enthused as the rest of the crowd.

"Isn't this wonderful?" she was literally beaming from ear to ear. It was infectious and Daisy, Helena and the children were soon smiling and skipping around with the rest of them. The first stop was the toilets, it had been a long drive and Helena was bursting. As with the parking, there were huge queues so Daisy decided that they must all try to go. One of the complications of the breakdown in her nuclear family was the toilet scenario. Cory was not impressed to have to go in the girls toilets but bearing in mind that they had waited so long here and Daisy was not willing to wait any longer he urelented. Also she never liked sending her child into the toilet alone, there were far too many horror stories of weird things happening to children in toilets. However she had contemplated skipping the queue by taking him in there herself but there were even more horror stories about the state of mens toilets in general. Waiting would be fine.

After the palaver was over the five of them wandered off in the direction of the main attraction. Georgie was chatting with the children about how she loved the idea of the airshow because it didn't matter if you got stuck at the back of the audience because, like fireworks, they were going up in the air, so everyone would be able to see them. She then continued to tell Sally about a Status Quo concert she had once been to and couldn't see a thing because she was right at the furthest back corner of the stadium. Daisy had to quickly avert Sally's attention when Georgie starting telling her about how she had got high from all the dope being smoked around her. Thankfully it worked and Georgie hadn't suspected a thing. Cory was walking along swinging hands with Helena and they were discussing whether the aeroplanes would have bombs on board just in case they had to suddenly leave because there was a war somewhere.

Daisy meandered along behind them all, enjoying listening to them chatting. She was smiling contently at being out in the sunshine with the people she loved the most in the world, when seemingly out of nowhere her angel barman materialised.

"Hello you, how are you doing? I didn't know you were going to be here," exclaimed Daisy, hugging him and receiving a kiss on the check.

"Well I thought I can't miss out on one of the biggest events in Lincoln. Plus," he whispered conspiratorially, "I hear they serve a cracking bacon butty at that burger van over there."

Just as they were laughing about the trouble of trying to find a perfect burger or bacon butty, she heard Cory shout, "Daddy!"

She spun round to see Joel strutting towards them, burger in one hand and camera in the other.

"Small world," Daisy stated.

Both men smirked.

"So Joel, this is Stephan, Georgie's nephew. Stephan this is Joel, the children's Dad."

The men eyed each other for a moment.

Joel just stood awkwardly watching the interaction between Daisy and Stephan. His arms were rested on the children's shoulders in a protective man stance. *Here we go another alpha male moment.*

Daisy attempted to lighten the mood.

"So where is the best place for us to start?" he asked looking around.

Stephan picked up on her endeavour.

"Well over there they have a plane that the children can sit in, they might like that."

"Yes," jumped in Joel, "I think they would enjoy that. Shall I take them over?"

Lord, he was practically stating his claim on his children. Daisy rolled her eyes.

"Sure, we are heading for the coffee stand. I'll meet you back there, yes?"

She considered that if he was willing to trawl around then fabulous, it gave her a chance to recoup from the drive.

Stephan was chatting to Georgie and Helena. In fact, Helena was swooning in a way that Daisy had never seen before. Daisy gestured to them that she was going for coffee and left them to it. She contemplated how it was that they were all in the same place at the same time. They could not have planned it if they had tried.

Daisy settled herself into a chair next to the coffee stall. Everyone was pretty much scrambling for a seat. Luckily a friendly looking couple were leaving as she had arrived. The other spare seat was taken by a lady who looked thoroughly bored and as though she would be more than happy to spend the rest of the day cradling her coffee and letting the world go by. Or more to the point let her husband meander off by himself. Obviously this was not her kind of thing. She kept giving him reassuring looks as he called over to her about the things they could go and see. There were a lot of 'yes Dear' answers from her, but very little enthusiasm, even though she plastered on a smile every time so acknowledged him.

Daisy knew that she was obviously hugely committed to him, why else would she have even tagged along. Her husband bounded around like a child at a fayre and she reassured him. But her heart was not in it. Daisy considered whether her and Joel would have become those kind of people in years to come. As much as their sexual orientation differed they had always been good friends with similar interests. So on the occasions that they had attended similar events to this they had been equally enthralled. She considered that it was one of the reasons that they had in fact managed to stay together as many years as they had.

Obviously the children had helped to keep them together. They had been and still were a common interest to them both. They had both craved a family and were overjoyed when they had fallen pregnant, as much the second time as the first. As parents and friends they were very compatible. But as ever in these situations the 'elephant' in the room had finally had to be acknowledged for the issue that it was. Joel could never fully love her and neither of them could be satisfied within their marriage. She knew that their separation was the right thing to have done.

Watching him now talking with mutual friends, she still saw the man she had emotionally supported and who had supported her. She smiled to herself and the life they had shared and luckily; due to his bravery in being honest with her, they were still a big part of each other's lives. She was glad things had worked out well for them both. She hoped that the future held good things for them all. Seeing him now and knowing how she felt about her new life, she knew that life would hold happiness for both of them.

"Mummy, Mummy," Cory ran towards her, trying to catch his breath to tell her something, "the aeroplanes are going to start flying soon, can we go watch them?"

She picked up her belongings, "Of course we can honey."

Holding her son with one hand and her coffee and bag in the other, they made their way over to the others.

All of them walked towards where the planes were going to do the display. They were chatting and smiling and the children skipped around them. As Daisy caught Joel's eye he smiled at her, the beaming smile of a good friend who was thoroughly enjoying the moment. She returned the smile and then saw Stephan's hand brush his. It was such a fleeting gesture that she was unsure if her eyes were deceiving her but as Joel held eye-contact with her she realised she had in fact seen the contact between them.

Her heart skipped a beat and she caught her breath in her throat. Then a sudden recollection caused all of the pieces of the puzzle to fall into place. Joel turning up after a night out in Lincoln. Stephan and Joel seemingly recognising each other. Joel smiled at her as he took Stephan by the hand in a bold and confident move. A sure sign to one and all that they were a couple. A very comfortable with each other kind of couple. Somehow seeing Joel and Stephan together made Daisy realise that no matter what issues had arisen from their separation, it had been worth it. He was happy, thus so were the children. None of their group seemed to bat an eyelid, not even the children, who, as far as she knew, had not seen him with anyone since her.

Georgie sidled up beside her and linked arms; hugging her arm as she did so.

"How wonderful to see everyone so happy."

"It certainly is Georgie."

"Who would have thought it would have all worked out so fabulously."

"Indeed." Daisy beamed at the children as they both turned in their direction, huge smiles on their faces.

Daisy mused at how things really had worked out so well for all of them. Not so long ago, she was at the bottom of a pit of despair and confusion, yet now she was so happy and content in her world and all who shared her space. In all honesty she could not remember her life ever feeling quite as perfect as it did right now.

They all slowed to a stop as the planes started their flying displays. They cheered and clapped and squinted in the summer sun. Then as though in a scene from Top Gun, Tristan appeared from the gathering crowd, sunglasses on and a smile to match the warmth in her heart for him. Without even a second thought she trotted over to him and hugged him as if he had just returned from months away.

"Nice to see you too," he grinned.

December - Ups-a-Daisy

The weeks had passed quickly since Tristan's Mum had passed away. Daisy had done everything she could to be a pillar of support for him. She helped organise the paperwork, and the funeral (even to the point that she catered the Wake). Her Mum had been understanding at the times that she had had to call her to watch the children. Tristan had joined her to walk the dogs most days leading up to the funeral. Sometimes they chatted endlessly, other days they walked in silent contemplation. Tristan had needed the time away from work to heal his broken heart and Daisy tried her hardest to help. She understood that the grieving process was a very personal one, yet to have a friend to lean on was a welcome comfort or distraction, whichever fitted the need of the moment.

Equally Daisy had enjoyed his company, he was easy to be around. It seemed a strange thing to feel while he was so low in himself. But since his ego had been stripped away and he was just needing to get through each day and out the other side, there was a bizarre simplicity to him. His egotistical nature may have drawn the crowds but he rarely allowed people beyond the barrier that held strong. Daisy felt grateful to be around him at this time and see the young man she had once lived her life with and for. On odd occasions when he was stronger the children joined them. Their innocence and naivety to the situation somehow assisted in building him up and momentarily forgetting his angst.

On one of their walks, a few days before Christmas, Tristan and Daisy were wrapped up beyond recognition. Daisy's long scarf was one she had knitted years ago when she was pregnant with Sally. It was not the best knitting she had ever done but it was keeping her warm, as it wrapped around her neck three times and still reached her knees. Her coat was the same length and she was wearing her wellies. It was by no means her most attractive look. Although Tristan was not looking much more attractive in his wax jacket, wellies and woolly hat. They had four of the dogs with them; two each. The ones Tristan was holding were quite beastly, so Daisy was pleased to have his help.

There had been a thick frost the night before, which lay heavy and sparkling in the brightness of the sun. Christmas was in the air and today felt as though it had arrived for sure. Daisy loved this time of year; the children were excitable and the dusty decorations had been brought down from the loft. More than the commercial side, which she hated, it felt as though magic was in the air, possibly carried with the frost and sprinkled across the leafless trees and sparse fields. They both squinted slightly as they turned the corner to walk along the dirt track that ran behind the houses. Daisy felt her energies replenishing, as the chilled air filled her lungs and the sun beamed down upon her. She could almost see the same thing happening to Tristan; the tension in his face had seemed to have been there forever, ebbed away as nature took hold of him in her mothering embrace.

"I am sorry by the way."

"How do you mean?"

"About the bear." His head dropped slightly. "I couldn't let it go. I had to let the baby go and then you. I needed something to hold on to. But I buried it with Mum, she'll keep it safe."

Daisy allowed a tear or two to roll down her cheeks. They walked along in silence for a bit. There was nothing to be said. The past had been laid to rest. They were now looking to the future.

"Thank you," he said as the dogs suddenly tugged him a few steps ahead of her, having spotted a pheasant nearly.

"What for giving you the wee beasties?" she laughed.

"No, you wally," he chuckled, "I wasn't being sarcastic for once. I meant thank you for all your help lately. It is much appreciated you know."

Daisy was taken aback. She blushed slightly, but it was hardly noticeable as her cheeks and nose were already rosy from the bitter chill.

"You are more than welcome. It was nothing I wouldn't have done for anyone else."

"Don't brush it off," the dogs pulled him further away and he had to turn to be heard, "I know you went above and beyond the terms of friendship. I really..." they pulled him with a huge jolt as they lurched to chase a pheasant across the field. It was taking all his strength to hold on to them, "am grateful." He shouted back to her.

She had to stop because she was laughing so much. The beasties were practically dragging him in the direction of the pheasant, which was now moving very fast to escape the barking hounds. Daisy's two little pugs just looked up at her as though asking why the other dogs were acting so crazy. Once his dogs calmed down Daisy jogged slightly to catch him up. He was bent over, out of breath and his dogs were still keeping an eye out for their prey. At any moment they would charge at even the slightest chance of catching it. Daisy put her arm around his back and leant over to ask if he was ok. As she did he turned and looked her straight in the eye.

"I was serious Daisy, I thank you from the bottom of my heart. I would not have made it through all this if you had not been there to catch me as I fell."

As though taking his words literally, the beasties set off at full speed towards a moving bush on the other side of the field. Daisy fell backwards and landed hard on her bottom, her pugs luckily moved just in time. Tristan was also thrown backwards and dragged on his back through the field of sprouting corn. Daisy did not know quite how they would explain this to either the farmer or the owner of the dogs who were coated in thick mud. Thankfully she did not have to take back two squashed pugs, they were very happy that Daisy was now at ground level because it meant that they could climb all over her with their tiny muddy paws and give her lots of kisses. Daisy just relented. There was no point trying to fight it. Tristan would be a while trying to get his dogs back under control and untangling himself from their leads which, miraculously, he had managed to keep hold of.

Daisy and Tristan where now safely back at her house. The dogs had been returned home and both of them had since showered and their clothes and coats were currently in the washing machine. Their wellies stood on the front doorstep, ready to be dealt with later. They were both cradling a cup of hot chocolate. Daisy was wearing her grey trackies and red hoody, and Tristan was fashioning her purple dressing gown. It had been difficult for her to keep a straight face as he walked out in it. On her it almost reached her ankles, on him it just covered his knees. He looked vulnerable in it somehow, she wanted nothing more than to offer that he take it off but that would not only be inappropriate but her house was still warming up. She imagined never washing it again, just because he was wearing it, yet corrected her lurid thoughts. She had seen him naked many times before but that was a very long time ago and whether it was her animal instincts kicking in, or Georgie's crudeness rubbing off, she didn't know. But something very overwhelming made her want to just whisk him off to her bedroom.

However, her responsibilities saved her from herself, she glanced at the clock and realised she was going to be late for the school run.

"Are you ok here while I go pick up the kids? I'd offer to take you with me, but it is cold outside, plus you might get mobbed by lots of lonely housewives."

He smiled over his mug, "I'm fine, do you want me to pop the clothes in the tumble dryer if they finish while you are gone?"

"Erm, yea, that would be fab." Not only was she taken aback by his offer, but extremely conscious that her underwear was in there too, the mud had literally gotten everywhere. It crossed her mind that he might also have his in there too and she blushed again. Turning away she fetched her coat and trainers and headed out. *Had it really been that long without sex that she was blushing at his underwear being in her washing machine. Or was it more the thought that he was actually naked in her dressing gown. 'Behave yourself'* she chastised herself.

Daisy was pleased to be handed another mug of hot chocolate on her return home. Tristan had also made one for the children, with marshmallows floating on the top. Daisy and the children thanked him and sipped them gratefully. *So this*, thought Daisy, *was the kind of thing she missed by not having a man about the house*. Not that she remembered Joel ever doing such thoughtful things for them. Cory was laughing hysterically at Sally who had a thick marshmallow moustache. Luckily she was in a good mood today, and she pulled funny faces at him to make him laugh harder. Daisy had realised that the children laughed a lot more these days, and thinking about it, so did she. Although the last few months were tarnished with Tristan's grief, in a strange way he had brought happiness and comfort into their lives too.

As she stood watching the children, a contented grin on her face, she became aware that Tristan was watching her. She turned and smiled at him as his gaze fixed on her and he winked. Daisy's knees instantly melted and she had to lean against the worktop to steady herself. If there was one thing which could soften her resolve it was a man winking at her; especially if that man was Tristan. She pulled herself together and scooped past the children to the utility room. She busied herself checking the clothing situation, even though she knew they would not be dry yet. Just as she closed the tumble dryer door and turned it back on she heard the children chattering away to Tristan.

"So why…?" asked Sally, a big frown on her now marshmallow free face.

Daisy looked from Sally to Tristan and Cory mimicked her. Tristan looked at Sally and then at Daisy, who was now also frowning. He tripped over his words and looked to Daisy for support. She had obviously not heard the question so the only help she could offer was a shrug of her shoulders and a perplexed look.

"Well… I… I mean, we… erm…" he begged Daisy for help with his eyes.

"What's up Sally?" Daisy had to step in, if for no other reason than she was confused.

Sally looked up at her with innocent eyes, she looked as though she might burst into tears at any moment and Daisy moved closer to try to comfort her. She crouched down and asked her what was wrong. Daisy had forgotten how much pain she was still in from her fall, but crouching seemed to exacerbate the bruising.

"I just wondered why Tristan was wearing your dressing gown?"

Oh, no wonder Tristan was struggling. Daisy smiled reassuringly at her daughter.

"Well, we were out walking the dogs and Tristan got dragged across the field by the dogs and I got knocked over too, so our clothes got really muddy. Tristan didn't have anything else to wear so I offered him my dressing gown."

"Oh," the children chorused.

"So what happened?" Cory asked Tristan excitedly.

Tristan had broken out of his panic and the children and him sat around the table as he told the children all about the dogs and the pheasant, the children giggled away as the story got more thrilling. Daisy pottered about the kitchen preparing dinner and listening, butting in if he missed anything. Her heart yearned for these moments to last forever, the children happy and Tristan joining them for the afternoon, but she knew that reality was never as smooth running as this. These were rare moments, cherishable ones. If only life could be this wonderful all the time. However, she considered as she chopped the vegetables that life had been more of these moments lately than bad ones.

The year had been a good one, all things considered. Life had moved forward. She had come a long way. Things were actually very good. She had gotten back up after the adversity, like a daisy after the lawn has been cut. The bad moments were becoming the rare ones. She found herself giving a contented smile. Tristan and the children were all looking at her as she glanced up.

"What?"

They all laughed.

"It is so nice to see you happy Mummy," chirped up Cory. Sally and Tristan nodded in agreement.

"I was just thinking the same about you guys." She smiled the most genuine smile ever.

❀❀❀❀❀❀❀THE END❀❀❀❀❀❀❀

38801084R00136

Made in the USA
Charleston, SC
19 February 2015